C000241729

The
Wrong
Stuff

Guy Thair

A mysterious box opens a link to the past, revealing a plot to change the future...

When Hannah Meredith buys a box marked
"stuff" at an auction, her world suddenly
unravels into a series of increasingly
bizarre and terrifying events.

Follow Hannah and her unlikely allies in
their frantic attempts to stay alive and save
the world from disaster in The Wrong Stuff.
A fast moving, original thriller with a
scifi twist and more than a touch of black humour.

Indies United Publishing House, LLC
P.O. Box 3071
Quincy, IL 62305-3071
<u>www.indiesunited.net</u>

For my wife, Rhonda.
Who has always said nice things about my writing,
even when she didn't have to.

Table of Contents

1
A New Aquisition

Ever since her husband died five years before, leaving her a considerable but not exorbitant inheritance, Hannah Meredith developed a love for going to blind auctions. Just the thought of digging through piles of assorted junk and miscellany made her heart race. There was something almost magical about buying a mysterious, sealed box for a few quid and tearing it open to see if there were unrecognized treasures inside.

Of course, she wasn't usually that lucky. Mostly she found third-rate silverware, cracked and faded crockery, dusty electrical components, and obscure mechanical spare parts or, if you were really lucky, maybe some half-decent antique jewelry or a not totally, dreadful painting.

She was never going to make a living from her lucky-dip bidding, but Hannah wasn't ready to give up hope just yet. The Big Score might be the very next lot that went under the hammer, then how bad would she feel?

No, she felt perfectly justified in spending a hundred pounds or so every couple of months. It was hardly an extravagance after all, and she sold most of the items she had no use for online and at the garage sales she held twice a year to make way for new purchases.

The latest Aladdin's cave of dubious delights was an auction, only recently opened, in the upstairs room of a pub in a nearby village. She'd already been to three others this month, (usually her limit) so she initially resisted the temptation. But the closer the time came, the greater the feeling grew she would be missing out on something special. By the time auction day arrived, there was no question of her not going, convinced her fortune awaited, under the taped-down flaps of some anonymous cardboard box.

Hannah arrived early at the pub; a quaint, low-ceilinged place with a roaring fire in the hearth and walls covered in hunting paraphernalia and old black and white photographs of country life in days gone by. She bought herself a drink and wandered around the two small bars, inspecting the memorabilia of a community that probably had not changed all that much in two hundred years.

After a while, she noticed people beginning to arrive and head for the stairs in the back corner of the pub, so she drifted over until she could hear muted conversations in the room on the floor above.

"...some interesting items..."

"...going to raise serious money with those..."

"I don't think I've ever seen one as fine as this..."

Casually strolling over to the bar, she finished her drink and placed the empty glass on the oak counter, before turning to follow two more new arrivals up the stairs.

The atmosphere in the large open room was a strange mix of restrained excitement and almost spiritual reverence. Small groups of people gathered in tight circles, voices barely raised above a whisper, scattered around the sparely furnished room.

Nobody even registered Hannah's existence, let alone approached or spoke to her. Glancing around, she made for the largest, least crowded table in the center of the room, which seemed to attract only the merest of uninterested glances from most of the punters as they drifted around, eyeing the sale items and whispering to each other.

Inwardly pleased when she saw the battered selection of boxes on the table, with things like Bureau, Misc, and Basement written in marker, thinking there might be some surprises in those.

Then she saw the box she immediately, shockingly knew with absolute certainty she was going to buy. It was a medium sized box, the cardboard visibly older than most of the other boxes Hannah could see, but otherwise not remarkable in any way.

And on the side, in the same scrawl that marked the rest, one word, Stuff.

That was all. Not very descriptive, but then, that was the thrill, wasn't it? The not knowing was what made it exciting.

She suddenly became aware of a change in the room. The whispered conversations had tailed off, all movement had stilled and everyone turned to face the man who had just entered through the room's only other door.

"Ladies and gentlemen, welcome to the sale by auction of the estate of Marvin Calderwood. Please prepare to place your bids on any items that may have piqued your interest."

Hannah half-listened to the rest of the auctioneer's spiel while keeping a close eye on "her" box, scanning the room to see if anyone else was paying it too much attention. It appeared, however, she was the only one drawn to that particular lot and relaxed, content to observe the bidding and wait her turn.

"And now we come to lot number 37, a box, presumably containing miscellaneous items and simply labeled "Stuff". I'll start the bidding at fifteen, will somebody give me fifteen pounds?"

Hannah looked around nervously, about to raise her hand to bid, when she noticed nobody else seemed remotely interested. She looked back at the auctioneer, who looked around the room a few more seconds before finally asking, "Ok, who'll start me off at ten pounds? Ten pounds, anyone? No? Five, will anyone offer me five?"

Hannah couldn't bear it any longer and nearly jumped up in the air in her eagerness to secure the box. "Yes!", louder than she'd intended, "I'll have it. I mean, yes, five pounds, I'll bid five pounds."

"Five pounds I'm bid, any further bids? No, alright, at five pounds, lot 37 goes to the lady at the back."

2

Take the money or open the box?

"Miss?…Miss? Excuse me, Miss Hannah Meredith?"

She was so wrapped up in the auction it took a moment before Hannah realised the voice was addressing her. Turning to meet the politely inquiring, but somehow unnerving gaze, of a small, bird-like man with lank, greasy hair and strangely small, closely packed teeth, holding out a clipboard and a pen. The man's badge read Crowne Estate Auctions, and informed anyone unfortunate enough to need to know, he was called "Bronk", although Hannah found it difficult to believe this could be his first name.

"Yes, sorry, I was miles away."

"If you would just like to sign here," marking the relevant box with a neat cross, "and fill in your payment details. You can pick up your purchase on your way out."

Hannah mumbled a thank you, scrawled on the form and accepted a receipt from the strange little man before he scuttled away and she turned back to watch the auction.

Except, there was something different about the atmosphere in the room now, it felt tense all of a sudden.

And there seemed to be a pause in the bidding.

Then she noticed some of the other guests were looking at her.

All of them, in fact.

No, that wasn't right, shaking her head. Not looking at her, watching her was more like it. As if they were waiting for her to do something. What had the clerk said; "…pick up your purchase on your way out?"

Was that a not-so-subtle hint for her to leave? Were they waiting until she left before they would continue?

Hannah stared defiantly back at the group of vaguely threatening faces for a few seconds, just to show she wasn't to be intimidated so easily, *(which she was)* then turned and, as nonchalantly as she could, strolled over to the table nearest the door and presented her receipt to the silent, yet in some way disapproving, woman sitting behind it.

She looked briefly at the slip of paper, then glanced back up at Hannah, this time with a look of... what, surprise? curiosity? Hannah didn't know, but she did know she wanted nothing more than to grab her box of Stuff and get the hell out of there.

"Lot 37," she said, "it's that old cardboard box on the middle table, here you are."

She handed a crumpled five pound note to the woman, who took it with an expression that said she wished she had some tongs, or at least a pair of gloves, before signaling the oddly-named Bronk, who collected her box under the watchful, silent gaze of the assembled guests and carefully placed it on the table in front of her.

Hannah nodded coldly at the room in general, picked up the box and headed as quickly as dignity would allow down the stairs, into the reassuring warm coziness of the pub below. When glanced back, she caught sight of Bronk, sneering down at her as he closed the door to the upstairs room.

He paused when he saw her watching and said in a whisper, "Enjoy your purchase Miss Meredith, you've got a bargain there and no mistake."

"But, how do you...?" began Hannah, but the door closed on her question, and she heard the sound of a key turning in the lock, clearly indicating further discussion would not be forthcoming.

She bought another drink, her latest acquisition

perched on the neighboring stool at the empty bar, and reflected on the bizarre experience she'd just had. The thing was, she really had been quite scared for a minute back there, but she couldn't even begin to explain to herself why that was, let alone do so to anyone else.

Picking up the box and balancing her drink on top of it just long enough to cross the rug in front of the crackling log fire, she opened the door to the smoking area at the side of the building and went outside.

Sitting down, she leaned back on the rough stone wall, lit one of the thin cheroots her husband had hated so much and stared at the sealed and enigmatic cardboard box on the bench next to her. She was still sitting there lost in thought a few minutes later when the door to the bar opened and a tall, well-dressed man stepped out onto the small square of ash-stained paving slabs and clicked an expensive lighter. Although Hannah was surprised when she saw it lighting the ragged end of a rather inexpertly made roll-up, and the otherwise sophisticated-looking gentleman was having considerable difficulty getting it burning to his satisfaction.

Once he achieved full ignition, he took a couple of puffs, inhaled deeply and let out a huge cloud of smoke with audible relief. Then spoiled the effect by making disgusted spitting noises while picking flecks of tobacco from his mouth a few seconds later.

Hannah couldn't help it, she burst out laughing.

He looked down at her, fingers mid-grab seeking another errant strand inside his bottom lip, which made him look even more comical and Hannah laughed harder than ever.

He stubbed out his rapidly deteriorating cigarette in an ashtray and grinned back at her, held up one finger in the universal sign language of "Wait just a second" and turned his head to spit out one final unwanted piece of bitter vegetation.

She waited for him to recover his composure and then offered up one her cheroots, "Would you like one of mine?"

"No, I'd better not, thank you anyway. I quit last year, but I've gotten a bit of bad news and the barman was kind enough to give me that," he grimaced in the direction of the ashtray, "and I didn't like to ask him to make it for me."

"I had a slightly, umm, stressful experience just now too," said Hannah, "and, even though I can't claim I've ever quit, I certainly needed this one."

She took one last puff, dropped the stub next to his in the ashtray and was about to say something else when she noticed him staring at the box.

"You bought it!" he gasped, looking from her to the box and back again in amazement, "I thought… I mean, they told me…" He stopped, seemed to gather himself somehow, then calmly looked Hannah straight in the eye and asked her in an urgent voice, "Have you opened it yet?"

"What? The box? No, I… I only just got it. At the auction upstairs. They aren't very friendly up there though, I warn you. Although," looking at his tailored jacket and immaculately knotted tie, "you might be more their cup of tea I suppose."

He smiled in a distracted way, before turning more serious, "I'd like to buy it from you. Right now. What did you pay for it? I'll give you double."

"Erm, really? I'm not sure I want to sell it, I don't even know what's in here yet."

He blinked, "I'm so sorry, how rude of me, I haven't introduced myself," holding out his hand, "Paul Forrester, pleased to meet you."

She shook his hand, "Hannah, Hannah Meredith." she said, "That's ok, you're obviously having a bad day and I'm dreadful with names anyway," she laughed again, "memory like a sieve."

"So,", all business again, "how would you like to make a quick profit on your box of old junk?" Flashing her a quick encouraging grin, but was still clearly expecting an affirmative answer.

This is getting strange again, thought Hannah, I think it may be time to make my excuses and leave. Out loud, she said, "I'll tell you what, do you have a card? Wait until after I've gotten home and had a look at what's inside, then I'll know whether I want to sell it or not. If I do, you'll be the first to know. How's that?"

"I'll give you a thousand pounds, here and now. Cash." Reaching into his jacket and bringing out a bulging wallet, from which he extracted a thick wad of fifty pound notes. He then made a show of counting out twenty of the crisp notes onto the table and placing his hand on top of the pile. "Box unopened, no questions asked, one time offer. What do you say?"

"I'm sorry, I'm going to stick to what I said," eyeing the stack of cash regretfully. The voice in her head, however, had other ideas, crying out, are you mad!? That's £1,000 there, you fool, think of all the other boxes of stuff you could buy with that!

But what came out of her mouth was a little more tame. "I promise I'll call you if you give me your number. I give you my word as a fellow junk hunter."

This completely failed to raise a smile, in fact Forrester was becoming more agitated by the second and seemed about to launch into another appeal, so Hannah stood up, tucked the box under her arm and stepped back into the warm, woodsmoke-scented pub, placing her empty glass on the nearest table as she made for the front door. More than ready to leave this night, and Forrester, behind her.

He caught up with her in the car park.

"Miss Meredith? I apologize, I didn't mean to upset you," stopping a few paces from her, hands held out in a conciliatory gesture, "here, take my card as you suggested, I'll wait to hear from you."

Handing her a classy, heavily embossed business card with just his name and a phone number. "My private number," he said, "call me anytime, day or night, ok?"

She nodded. He held her gaze for a few seconds and seemed to decide something, nodded in return and headed back inside the pub, leaving her alone in the silent car park.

It was only as she drove home did it occur to Hannah that people had been calling her "Miss" all evening, even though she'd never met any of them before, and she did not yet have the courage to remove her wedding ring, despite having reverted to her maiden name since her husband's death.

How did they know? It was just another odd detail to a very strange evening indeed, and all the strangeness made her even more keen to get her purchase home and find out what the mysterious box contained.

3
Moment of Truth

Hannah sat in the kitchen, listening to her late husband's expensive coffee machine making asthmatic wheezing noises on the worktop behind her, while she stared at the box on the table.

Beep.

A simple electronic noise which, nonetheless, managed to sound imperious and superior, informing her a minuscule thimble-full of horribly bitter and overpriced coffee was ready to burn herself on. After retrieved the bitter brew from the fiendish machine with only minimal second-degree scalding, she sat down to gaze absently out of the window at the fields behind the farmhouse, going over the evening's bizarre events in her head.

She was more intrigued than ever to find out what her mystery purchase would turn out to be, but after the inordinate amount of interest shown by the equally mysterious Mr. Forrester, she was also nervous about discovering what opening the box might reveal.

Hannah took a last mouthful of eye-watering coffee, shuddered, and tipped the rest down the sink before carrying the box into the living room. She paused to place it on the coffee table before heading to the living room bar to pour herself a much needed real drink.

Taking a couple of fortifying gulps of gin with a hint of tonic, she leaned forward and ripped the tape from the top of the box marked *"Stuff"*, and slowly folded back the soft, much-handled cardboard to look inside.

Her heart sank.

Was this it?

Hannah reached in and took out a yellowed envelope tucked under the lid, turning it over a few times to confirm it was sealed with no writing of any kind on it anywhere and laid it aside. Carefully tilting the box on its side, she tipped the remainder of the box's contents onto the table, making sure she didn't lose any of the smaller, unfamiliar components.

Because that was clearly what they were.

Component parts of a larger object.

Like a kit, she mused, like all those model cars Barney used to make when we were kids...

Barney was her older brother, now living in South Africa, married to a goldmine heiress and disgustingly rich, had been a regular little mechanical engineer when they were younger, building scale models of all sorts of things, with working gears and motors and electronic components. There were gears and motors here too, along with what appeared to be a clock-face and an old fashioned telephone dial, some very basic-looking headphones and a lot of neatly wound lengths of wire.

The rest of it, Hannah could only guess at, and even then she was pretty confident she'd guess wrong.

The box itself was obviously very old, just the feel of the cardboard told her that. She'd become quite the connoisseur of antique packaging since she'd been bitten by the auction bug, and the strange kit of parts, although they appeared brand new, had a vintage look; as if a designer from the past was imagining what futuristic technology would look like.

After inspecting a few of the more easily identifiable parts for a few minutes and finding herself none the wiser, Hannah turned her attention to the unaddressed envelope beside the now empty box. The paper felt stiff and was discoloured by age, but the flap was still glued down firmly and had obviously never been opened since the box had been sealed, presumably many years before.

With only a brief pause, and a fleeting stab of what... foreboding? Hannah tore the end off the envelope and tipped out a single sheet of folded paper along with a small handmade booklet for what appeared to be assembly instructions for the world's most complicated clock.

Unfolding the paper revealing a page of closely spaced, fastidiously neat handwriting in faded blue ink, with old-fashioned cursive characters Hannah hadn't seen since she'd attended the dusty old boarding school her parents had farmed her off to for the best part of, if you could call it that, her childhood.

There was no address on the letter, it simply began; "*My dear unknown and unfortunate accomplice...*"

Which, quite frankly, was not the kind of letter you could easily put aside to read later, it sort of demanded you pay attention right there and then, so Hannah got up, poured herself another generous G with no T, settled back on the sofa, took a steadying gulp and started to read.

4
Trouble in Store

"My dear unknown and unfortunate accomplice, I feel I must, before anything else, apologize for the rather serious inconvenience you are almost certainly about to be put to. I can only hope that this brief note will go some way towards explaining the unenviable position in which you suddenly find yourself.

It is just as important that you understand why these events will occur, as it is to know how to avoid them and hopefully survive the oncoming assault on your life.

I do not tell you these things in order to frighten you (although only a fool would not fear those who now pursue you), but more as a way of preparing you to combat the dark forces ranged against you, whilst still having a chance of emerging victorious."

Hannah raised her eyes from the old letter and reached a hand that trembled ever so slightly for the glass on the coffee table. She took a thoroughly unladylike gulp, followed by a deep breath, then looked back down at the neat lines of handwriting and continued reading;

"I can only assume that you have recently come into possession of a box of components, probably at the sale of my estate, and I think I can also safely assume that you are ignorant as to their origin or purpose.

I can easily furnish you with the answers to questions you may have, indeed these are the very facts you require to assist you, but it is up to you alone to decide the veracity of my information, for nobody else is to be trusted in this matter, NOBODY.

It is vital you believe what I tell you, if you doubt anything at all, even for a moment, you will be lost.

I am writing this letter in the year eighteen hundred and forty-two and if you have gained possession of the box by legitimate means, then the envelope will have remained unopened since I sealed it a few minutes from now (please excuse this tortured use of tenses, you'll appreciate my difficulty soon enough) and you may have a few hours head start to allow you to prepare.

I have no way of knowing precisely when you are reading this, but I do know it must be after nineteen hundred and eighty-seven because that was the last time I saw the box you now possess..."

Hannah read the last sentence again, then went back and checked... "1842 and...yes, 1987, but that would make him well over a hundred..." Shaking her head, this just didn't make any sense.

"...which brings me to the point where you will, for the moment at least, have to take me at my word.

Three years ago, just before Christmas of 1839, I was conducting closely guarded experiments into the possible uses for a new discovery; electricity.

I had been a mechanical engineer for many years and I was contacted by someone from the government and asked to take part in a secret project to harness the almost limitless power of "tamed lightning".

They required someone to build a generator, one of such a size that it had yet to be even attempted by their designers and they had heard of my work on electric motors, inspired by the great Mr. Faraday, so I was retained to construct it for them.

The initial mechanical prototypes of the generator were successful and we were running a series of performance tests on the first working model when the original "incident" occurred.

Even now I cannot provide an adequate explanation for what transpired, except to say that the enormous power generated in those early experiments must have in some way distorted the very fabric of creation, in a way that made it possible for the usually linear nature of the world's history to become more elastic and malleable. Not only that, it became apparent that these distortions would allow a man to gain entry into parts of history that have yet to manifest themselves in our realm of being."

"Ok," Hannah muttered to herself while reaching for the last mouthful of drink in her glass and draining it, "this is going beyond a joke, is this guy talking about time travel here?"

Taking another deep breath, she was about to resume reading when she heard a noise out in the garden, the clattering sound of flower pots being knocked over, making her jump and glance nervously outside. Her reflection stared back at her from the black mirror of the living room window. Putting the letter on the coffee table and placing her empty glass on top of it, she stood up and grabbed the poker from the fireplace before making her way to the back door, where she gathered her courage before stepping out into the garden.

"Hello? Is there anybody there? I am armed you know, you don't want to mess with me."

Silence.

She took a look around and listened until she was sure there was nothing more to hear and turned to go back inside when she noticed a broken pot and footprints in the flower bed, right outside the living room window.

Someone had been watching her!

Hannah hurried into the house and slammed the door, throwing the bolt and leaning her back against it, where she stood shaking for a minute before a terrible thought occurred to her and she rushed into the living room and stopped in her tracks

The single sheet of yellowed paper was still where she had left it only minutes before.

But the box and its mysterious contents were gone!

5
Run

Hannah took a few steps towards the middle of the room, glancing around her nervously in case the intruder was still there. The shock of discovering her home had been invaded made her heart race and she noticed, in a detached sort of way, that she was shaking from the adrenaline rush.

She bent to retrieve the letter, slipping the sheet of paper out from under her glass just as she caught a movement from the corner of her eye and spun round in fright.

She found herself face to face with a man in evening dress, wearing what, in less traumatic circumstances would have looked ridiculous, the kind of small black mask worn by comic-book villains or the Lone Ranger, but in her current state of panic he looked terrifying.

Backing away from him, the backs of her legs came up against the low coffee table after only two shuffling steps. He grinned in what Hannah could only think of as a predatory way, as he locked his eyes on hers and took a step towards her.

With another jolt of adrenaline, she realised she still held the heavy iron poker in her hand and raised her arm in what she hoped was a threatening manner. "Get out of my house! I don't know what you want but if you don't leave right now you'll be sorry!"

She thought this show of defiance deserved a small display of fear on the part of her unwelcome visitor, or at the very least some sign of uncertainty, but all it achieved was to widen his grin as he suddenly made to snatch the letter from her.

To Hannah's great surprise, her immediate reflex action was to bring down the hand holding the poker in a swift chopping motion. She heard a loud snapping sound as it connected with his forearm seconds before he shrieked in pain.

"You fucking bitch, I'm going to 'ave you for that!" he snarled, holding his useless right arm close to his side. Reaching awkwardly into his jacket with his left hand, he brought out a wicked-looking knife which sprang opened with a nasty little "snick" noise, the long narrow blade catching the light as he swung it in a rapid arc towards Hannah's throat.

Stumbling, she lost her balance as the table skidded back under her weight but still swung wildly with the poker in a desperate attempt to fend off the lethal attack.

This time, the noise that accompanied the sudden impact of her weapon on something solid was far more unpleasant and Hannah felt, as well as heard, the sickening crunch as the curved end of the iron poker struck her unknown assailant squarely in the face.

She just managed to prevent herself from falling backwards at the last moment, as the poker wrenched her forward before sliding from her hand when the masked man collapsed like a puppet with its strings cut. The hooked iron rod dangling gruesomely from the ugly hole where his nose used to be, blood gushing from the wound like a fountain.

"Oh-my-god-oh-my-god-OH-MY-GOD!"

Staring at the spreading pool of blood and shaking like a leaf, she took huge, wracking gulps of air, letting them out in near-hysterical sobs as the urge to vomit almost overwhelmed her.

Then her legs seemed to catch up with what had been going on and promptly folded up, unceremoniously dumping her tailbone onto the hard edge of that bloody table. A bolt of pain shot up her spine, making her see stars and starting her eyes watering, but it seemed to act as a mental slap round the face, bringing her emotions back under control and relegating her rising terror to the background for the time being, allowing Hannah to concentrate on the situation at hand once more.

She gingerly got to her feet, wincing at the protest being registered by her throbbing back and it was only then that she noticed, in the mirror on the far side of the room, a thin red line and some smeared streaks on the left side of her neck.

She moved closer, looked at her disheveled reflection and suddenly felt sick all over again. The tip of the mysterious grinning man's knife must have just grazed her throat before she'd managed to bring him down.

Turning to look down at the pale, bloodied figure, lying motionless in front of the couch. Those cushions will need dry cleaning, she thought vaguely. her initial horror at what she'd done faded somewhat.

This man had intended to kill her!

What could possibly be in her box that was important enough to kill for?

And where was the box now?

Then she spotted it.

It was on the floor by the door leading to the hallway, the intruder had obviously gotten that far before Hannah returned and disturbed him.

"First things first though," Hannah announced to the otherwise empty house in a voice she was surprised to note was quite steady. She carefully picked up and closed the flick knife, before turning her attention to its owner, "Let's see if you're still alive shall we?"

She crouched down and pulled off the man's mask, dislodging the gore-covered poker, it slid free with a horrible sucking sound and rolled under the couch.

Admittedly it was difficult to tell, what with the blood

and the recent nose removal, but Hannah could have sworn this was one of the stuck-up and unfriendly punters who had been giving her the evil eye at the auction.

She pressed her fingertips to his throat, found a faint but regular pulse there, also noticing with some distaste, a slight bubbling in the unconscious man's brand new nasal orifice, enough to know she hadn't killed him anyway. But he wouldn't be out forever.

Looking around the blood-spattered living room until she found what she needed, a pair of her long woolen hiking socks draped over the fireside log basket to dry. Retrieving them, she returned to the stranger and used them tightly tie his hands behind his back, and his ankles together, before finally using his own tie to gag him with.

She rolled him onto his side to stop him choking on the blood that dribbled from his broken face and stood up.

When the mirror behind her exploded.

Hannah spun and saw the frame, with a few shards of glass still hanging around the edge, the rest were scattered over the carpet and frowned.

Then she saw the hole in the window

What the..?

Something that sounded like a mosquito on amphetamines shot past her right ear, a vase on the bookshelves exploded and it clicked, someone was shooting at her!

Hannah threw herself flat on the floor, bringing her face to face with her attacker once more, as more bullets zipped through her window, smashing ornaments and shredding books, filling the air with a shower of paper confetti.

She crawled frantically over the increasingly red, rather squishy, deep pile of her previously spotless living room carpet until she reached the hallway door, stopping just long enough to grab the box and cram the crumpled letter into it before she wriggled out into the hall. Shielded from this new attacker, she stood up and grabbed the car keys from their hook.

Since the shooting seemed to only be coming from the back of the house, she figured she had at least a few seconds before anyone found out she'd escaped. Taking a deep breath, and clutching the box under one arm, she opened the front door, quickly looked around, and ran as fast as she could for her late husband's mid-life crisis on wheels, his precious Porsche 911, parked under the carport beside the house.

She silently eased open the car door and slipped into the driver's seat, just as she heard voices behind her through the open front door.

"She isn't here, check outside…"

Hannah didn't wait any longer, she twisted the key in the ignition, threw it into reverse and gunned the engine, kicking up a spray of gravel as she spun out of the parking bay and turned up the driveway.

She heard shouting behind her, then the flat report of a gunshot and her wing mirror exploding into glittering pieces as she skidded out onto the road, the box and its enigmatic letter rattling around on the seat next to her as she stomped on the accelerator and fled into the night.

6
A Voice from the Past

Hannah kept her foot on the floor until she'd taken at least two corners at speeds that were more terrifying than the thought of what was behind her and finally eased up on the Porsche's accelerator before she did the assassins' job for them.

Keeping one eye permanently on the rear-view mirror, she made a quick inventory of her available resources. There was always cash in the glove box, after all, she never knew when she might need it to buy a bargain in a sale that would result in her being chased around the countryside by armed maniacs! Immediately realising this train of thought was counter-productive, Hannah took a slow, deep breath to calm herself before continuing with her mental inventory.

She usually kept a spare prepaid mobile phone in the car and noticed with relief that it was plugged into its charging cord under the dash. There was also a long winter coat, a folding shovel and a set of jump leads on the back seat. Tony, her late, barely-lamented husband would have gone apeshit if he'd known how she treated his beloved sports car. She'd crammed a bale of hay onto the leather upholstery more than once since his passing.

The box and the crumpled, rather grubby looking letter were on the seat next to her, she noticed both were streaked with blood, but otherwise seemed reasonably intact. The flick knife she'd taken from her newly noseless attacker was in her pocket. And apart from the clothes she had left the house in, a lighter and her tobacco tin, that was the sum total of her on-the-run survival kit.

Hannah slowed the car as she approached a junction, turning onto the bypass that lead northward, realized her internal auto-pilot was taking her in the direction of their, or rather *her*, she corrected herself wryly, holiday cottage by the lake.

Of course! The lake house would be a perfect place for her to lay low and try to work out what the hell was going on. She put her foot down once more and sped on, past silent woodland and moonlit, open fields, suddenly more determined now that she had a purpose.

It was almost an hour before she spotted the swinging wooden sign that said "Black's Lodge", the paint faded, the name and Gothic lettering a throwback to some previous owner which had never seemed worth changing. She swung into the drive, carefully navigating the dark and rutted track until it opened into a clearing that separated the lake shore from the front of the cottage.

Parking by the side of a low stone outbuilding, Hannah got out of the car and grabbed the box from the passenger seat, and headed towards the house. Climbing the steps of the porch, she took the key from its hiding place in the eaves, beneath the overhanging thatched roof. She paused, listening to the sounds of the woods and the gentle lapping of the lake, reassuring herself nothing was out of the ordinary before unlocking the door and going inside.

It didn't take her long to get a fire lit, there were always logs in the fireplace and kindling in a basket - although she felt a strange shudder go through her as she picked up the poker for the first time - and once the place felt more like home, she took the letter from the top of the Stuff box and smoothed it out on the kitchen counter, pulled out a stool and after finding her place, resumed reading.

"...Not only that, it became apparent that these distortions would allow a man to gain entry into parts of

history that have yet to manifest themselves in our realm of being.

I'm aware that these claims may sound extraordinary and even insane, but please be patient, the proof is in your hands.

If you have the small pamphlet that was enclosed with this letter, then you have all the directions required to construct the device from the components I have provided. The quicker you can achieve this, the quicker I can instruct you in the operation of the infernal device itself.

I urge you not to waste a moment more and to commence assembly of the device at your earliest opportunity, for only knowledge of its operation can improve the chances of eluding your pursuers.

I hope to communicate with you more directly in the near future.

> *Your apologetic co-conspirator,*
> *Marvin Calderwood."*

Hannah frowned, turned the paper over to check there was nothing more she'd missed and then laid it aside. Picking up the handwritten booklet she opening it to the first page.

It was simpler than she had first thought, assembling the strange components from the series of precise diagrams. Each item was colour-coded, making the process very straightforward. Once each gear was slotted into corresponding fittings on a panel it had the same, not-quite-familiar look, of something that *looked* like a circuit board, but one made by someone who had never actually seen one. The peculiar clock face/telephone dial component was attached last and Hannah looked thoughtfully at the final result.

"Well Marvin, I have no idea what this thing is, but it looks like the picture, so I think I put it together right. Big brother Barney would be proud of me." Congratulating herself aloud.

The final component in the box looked like an ordinary phone cable adapter, the sort that split one line into two, and Hannah unplugged her house phone, plugging it into the adapter and then inserted it back into the wall socket. All that remained was to plug the odd-looking contraption into the other socket on the adapter, which she did, then sat back on the sofa and admired her handiwork.

Then the phone rang.

She almost dropped her drink in shock.

Almost.

Hannah stared at the mysterious device, wincing at the harsh ringing but unable to tear her eyes from the switch on the small indicator panel which read "Answer".

Her hand trembling ever so slightly, she placed her glass on the arm of the sofa and picked up the receiver of the house phone.

There was an eerie hollowness to the silence on the line, but nothing else.

Hannah's throat suddenly felt horribly dry and she swallowed with difficulty before she could speak.

"Hello."

Nothing.

"Hello, is there anybody there?"

With an almost imperceptible change in the quality of the silence on the other end, she heard, "*Hello, this is Marvin Calderwood, I'm very pleased to make your acquaintance. Now, listen very carefully, you don't have very much time…*"

7
Time after Time

"Wait, what, you're Marvin Calderwood? But you're dead…aren't you..?" Hannah tailed off into bewildered silence realizing it was a pretty dumb question, all things considered.

Then she reconsidered, and she decided given the night's events so far, she had every right to ask a dumb question or ten and was about to ask a few more when the metallic sounding voice on the phone interrupted her before she could pick one.

"I'm sorry to spring all this upon you without any preamble madam, but there really is no time for pleasantries at this juncture. Time is, haha," he gave a strange, humourless bark of laughter, *"of the essence as they say and we shall have to save the formal introductions until a more convenient time."*

"Well, you can stop calling me "madam" for a start," belatedly noticing it was a rather frosty reply, "I'm not lady of the manor."

"My apologies, Mrs..?" he paused expectantly.

"Meredith, Hannah Meredith," she said, "I bought a box of your stuff at an auction tonight," looking at the clock above the fireplace she saw it was nearly 2 a.m. and corrected herself, "last night, and people have been trying to kill me ever since!" She took a deep breath. Could it really only be a few hours since this nightmare began?

"That is why it is vital that you hear what I have to say before the hunters pick up your trail again."

Calderwood, if it was indeed who the voice belonged to, spoke in a no nonsense tone that made Hannah even more nervous than she already was.

"Because although it is, of course, up to you to decide whether to assist me, they will not make that distinction. You will already have been marked for elimination. I'm sorry, I wish it was not the case but they will not allow witnesses to remain alive."

"Witnesses! Witness to what? I haven't seen anything, I don't know anything!" Hannah could feel herself starting to panic, "They can have the fucking box, I don't care, as long as they leave me in peace!" There was a pause and Hannah thought she heard a tut of disapproval.

"That would be very unwise Mrs. Meredith," his tone turning chilly, *"and I don't think there is any need for a lady to use such language, whatever the situation in which she finds herself."*

He actually sounded quite shocked, thought Hannah, which seemed unreasonably prudish, under the circumstances. "Call me Hannah, for fuck's sake," and grinned maliciously at the sharp intake of breath that came from the receiver, "and I told you, I'm not a lady."

Then a thought occurred to her and she felt a sudden, sickening lurch in her stomach, like an attack of vertigo, only much, much worse. "Where... I mean *when* are you calling from?" she asked, really, really not wanting to know the answer, "If you're Marvin Calderwood, you'd be ancient by now, so..."

"Ah, I see you are, despite your appalling manners," another pause and a disdainful sniff, *"at least bright enough to have made some deductions of your own. Yes, you are right to ask when and not where I am calling from, a fact I am grateful for as I have no time to convince you of that part of my story. I am, as I suspect you have already guessed, sitting at my desk in 1842, over one hundred and fifty years in your past,"* after a brief pause, he continued, *"Oh, would you be so kind as to tell me the date where you are now?"*

"What? Date? Um, 2016," almost whispering the date as her mind whirled with unanswered questions, "two hundred years ago, but..but, how?"

"I assume you read my letter, so you will know about the secret experiments. Well, this device is a direct result of my work on those vast generators. The rift I wrote of in that letter; the tear in creation through which I visited your accursed time, it also permits the use of the chronophonic device on which we are conversing. Indeed, communication is now all that it allows and if you choose to help me, soon that too will cease to be the case."

"Ok, you're going to have to back up a bit here Marvin, or whatever your name is," she was getting cross now and it made her feel better, "you visited my time? You mean you're a time traveller? Some sort of Victorian Doctor Who with a magic telephone and a tame wormhole?" Hannah burst into a fit of giggles. All the tension and stress of the previous night was taking its toll, she was dangerously close to getting hysterical and the phrase "tame wormhole" seemed hilariously funny for some reason.

After a minute or two, the giggles subsided and she was left feeling drained but more relaxed and wasn't surprised to notice she'd been crying. She wiped her eyes and blew her nose, then picked up the receiver from where she had dropped it.

"Hello, are you still there? I'm sorry about that, it's all just been a bit much, that's all."

"I quite understand Mrs...Hannah," Marvin replied. *"I expect it was the shock, you have been through an ordeal. If you are ready, I shall finish my story, after that you are free to do as you see fit."*

"Ok," said Hannah, switching on the phone's speaker and sitting back on the sofa, "I'd like to hear why my life has been turned upside down."

"After the rift was first discovered, forced open by the

immense power of the generators, I volunteered to investigate further and when I approached the area affected by the distortion I lost consciousnes. When I eventually came to, I had been ripped from my time and flung across the pages of history, to arrive in the year of 1976. I can only tell you it was a terrible shock and I shall spare you the details of the first few days, suffice to say I was sure I had lost my mind.

It was soon after this that I met the man of whom you should be most afraid; the despicable Mr. Paul Forrester."

Hannah was startled to hear the name again so soon. Wasn't he the man who had approached her after the auction and offered to buy her unopened box? "Yes, I've met him already, he wanted your device, I'm sure of it. He was very insistent, I think he might have been one of the men who came to the house."

"Oh I am certain that he was, he is a truly evil man and it is him we must stop at all costs," Calderwood said urgently. *"You must understand, I made a terrible mistake when I found myself trapped in your time, I put those that I hold dear in mortal danger. When I realized that I was unable to return to my own place in history I became demoralized and lonely and I thought to seek out my family."*

Hannah heard a catch in Calderwood's voice and he took a moment to regain his composure, but when he continued it was replaced by a hard edge of anger. *"I tracked down my descendants you see, my great-granddaughter and her family, and after I finally convinced her of the truth of my fantastical story they welcomed me into their home.*

I remained with them until I could exist in your time without difficulty, then found employment and soon paid back their generously many times over, for I could not have stayed sane without their loving company all those years. But now that we are separated once more, Forrester is using them to force me to take part in his evil scheme, by holding members of my family who are yet to be born! And there is nothing I can do about it."

8
Crime of the Century

"What do you mean, *evil scheme*, what exactly is Forrester planning to do?" asked Hannah. "How can he be holding people who aren't even...?" She stopped, the twisted logic of Calderwood's words suddenly sinking in. "You mean family who aren't born yet, *then*, don't you?" Running the sentence past herself a few times and realised what he meant about trouble with tenses.

"Yes, I am glad to see you are getting accustomed to the concept so swiftly, Mrs... I mean, Hannah." His words echoed tinnily back to her, via whatever mysterious connection was afforded by the old-but-new-looking "chronophonic device" she had assembled.

"Paul Forrester has taken my great-granddaughter's family as hostages, against my cooperation in a plan he hatched with others who knew about my work. A plan I had, Lord help me, already been a part of after I died, when those vultures..."

"Hang on, hang on, after you died? That can't be right, even from your point of view?"

"Forgive me madam, I mean Mrs. Hannah," Marvin was having a problem ditching the formality and she began to warm to him a little. *"You are right, it seems a trifle contrary, but I meant after I died, then, in your time, after my belongings were pawed through by those, those... scavengers."*

She could hear the bitterness in his voice.

"After they discovered the device you now have in front of you. That was when Forrester and his cohorts first conceived their grand scheme to rob the world."

"So you were already working with this bastard before I even bought the fucking box of doom!" She could almost see him wince and took pity on him. "Sorry Marvin, I'll try to be more ladylike. You were working with these villainous gentlemen prior to our unforeseen introduction?"

His laughter struck Hannah more like a release of tension than true amusement, but he sounded better for it. *"No need to apologize dear lady, your brusqueness is positively refreshing at times. And yes, to my shame, I allowed myself to be entrapped into assisting Forrester and his loathsome horde in an embezzlement, the likes of which you have never imagined."*

"So, if you were helping them, why did they bother kidnapping your family, I don't get it?" And it dawned on Hannah she was getting drawn into this fantastical tale; as if it were the most natural thing in the world to be talking to a man from two hundred years ago about murderous time-traveling kidnappers. "Unless... unless you somehow interfered with their scheme. Is that what happened, did you try to foil their cunning plan? Hahaha, I've always wanted an excuse to ask that."

"You could say that, yes. I will endeavour to explain, but we must be wary of the time, they will not take long to track you down..."

Marvin went on to explain how he had designed the timephone, as Hannah decided to call it, after carefully studying the wormhole and analyzing the information he was able to obtain with the very basic instruments available to Victorian scientists. Unfortunately, no matter how brilliant an engineer Calderwood had become and despite his growing understanding of how to utilize this new discovery, the materials and industrial processes required to actually manufacture his invention had yet to be even dreamed of.

So he had taken an extraordinary leap of faith by

allowing himself to be sucked, Hannah couldn't think of a better word, although the phrase "sucked by the wormhole" made her feel uncomfortable in a way she chose not to dwell on, through the rift into the present day, or rather the past of the present day, she'd given up trying to conjugate properly by now; where he had met his family.

Marvin then worked on inventing "new" technology to enable him to build the prototype of his device, which explained the future-retro look of the timephone, thought Hannah, he hadn't altered the look of his designs at all.

He then started to work on a replica of the generator that originally caused the rift, his hope being, if he could reproduce the original experiment precisely enough, he could reopen the wormhole corridor and one day use it to travel back and forth, visiting different points in history on the intervening timeline.

Then Paul Forrester walked into his office and his life changed forever. Again.

He was just an investor at first, that was all. But he showed such an interest in Marvin's work after a few years of working together, Marvin suggested they become partners. He felt Forrester could add his knowledge of computers and mass production techniques to Calderwood's inventive brilliance and unique experience of quantum mechanics to the benefit of both.

He considered Paul a trusted friend and confidant; the two of them ran a highly successful business together, consulting on and building everything from giant supercomputers for the London stock exchange to radio telescopes for the European Space Agency.

Then one evening while they were enjoying a quiet drink in Marvin's office, he decided to tell Forrester how he happened to be there. This was when the direction of his life changed course, the point at which it became inevitable that he'd end up where he was now, at the mercy of the man he had thought of as his closest friend.

Had Forrester been waiting for a moment like this, just hoping their friendship would give him a chance to steal his life's work from under his nose? Calderwood didn't know, but soon after his revelation, Forrester came to him with his idea.

"He wanted me to return to my own time and use the chronophonic device to communicate financial information to him." In an affronted voice, *"He was going to pass me the details of hugely successful inventions, processes, and companies from his past, but in my future."*

Hannah struggled to keep up.

"Then he would have me draw up designs and patents in his name so they could reap the benefits in the future. They wanted to hijack other peoples' life's work before they'd thought of it themselves. Fiendish, but he held a controlling interest in my company and he could have ruined me, exposed me and my discovery, anything to spite me, so I acquiesced to his demands."

Hannah's mind boggled at the thought of stealing the past but, if she accepted that all of this was even possible, which she guessed she was going to have to, what with the sudden increase in the number of murderous villains in her life, then she had to admit it seemed like an especially cunning plan.

"But now he and his cabal of unconscionable toadies have decided their wealth isn't enough for them, they want power too, so they are going to try and bring down the world economy and hold whole countries to ransom. Or maybe I should say that they are going to have tried to bring it down."

Hannah untangled the mass of mutilated grammar and gasped, "You mean they already did it, they were responsible for the crash? The credit crunch was their fault?"

"It's worse than that I'm afraid, that was merely a

rehearsal for the main event, so to speak, that is why they are so keen to stop the secret getting out."

Hannah was about to respond when she was interrupted by the sound of the cottage door opening. She spun around and, standing in the doorway, silhouetted by the headlights of a car she somehow managed not to notice arriving, was the looming figure of Paul Forrester.

"Hello again Miss Meredith." he grinned in what he probably thought was a suave manner, but it just made Hannah want to kick him in the balls.

"Bravo Marvin, a fine summing up of your situation." He clapped derisively in the direction of the timephone, as if Marvin could see and would appreciate the humour, "and yes, I'm afraid he's right, it's going to get worse. Much, much worse…"

9
Know Your Enemy

Forrester stood in the doorway, clearly expecting some sort of reaction to his unexpected arrival, so Hannah gave it to him.

"Even if I was easily intimidated, which I'm not, that sort of cheesy, cliché-ridden dramatic entrance was straight out of a fifties B-movie," she sneered at him and gestured at the timephone, "although maybe it isn't so odd, you've been spending so much time conspiring with Marvin here, you're losing your grip on modern social niceties."

Forrester just looked at her and smiled his supercilious smile. Then he spoke to someone outside the cottage in a low voice, closed the door and removed his long, expensive-looking coat, which he carefully draped over the back of a chair.

Turning to Hannah as if he was there visiting an old friend, Forrester asked in a cheerful voice, "So, what does a man have to do to get a drink around here then?"

Hannah bristled and very nearly said something that would have earned her a disapproving tut from Marvin. Giving him a hard stare, she relented after a moment and stood up, making for the drinks cabinet in the corner.

"No sudden moves or heroics please Miss Meredith," he warned, lowering himself into an armchair in front of the fire, "I really don't want to hurt you, so don't make me do something I'll regret, however briefly."

"That seems like a rather obvious lie, doesn't it," replied Hannah, "you've already tried to kill me once."

"A genuine mistake, I assure you," he confessed,

watching her splash cheap scotch into a tumbler; she'd be damned if he was getting the good stuff. "The man responsible has been disciplined and removed from the operation."

Hannah banged the drink down on the table next to his chair and retreated to the sofa, picked up her own glass.

"Pay him no heed my dear," Calderwood's words, tinny and metallic, nevertheless made her jump, spilling her drink on the carpet, *"the man hasn't an honourable bone in his body and wouldn't know how to be honest if you gave him lessons."*

"Ok Marvin, I'll bear that in mind," she said, "although I think I'm going to have to take him at his word for now, at least while he isn't actually trying to kill me."

"I admire your resolve madam, but be on your guard, he is as ruthless as he is charming."

Forrester sat and listened to this exchange with an amused look on his face, doing his best to disguise the look of distaste as he sipped his drink.

"Well, if that's all I have to worry about, I'll be fine," Hannah grinned nastily, "he's about as charming as genital warts."

To her delight, Marvin's affronted gasp was almost drowned out by the sound of Forrester choking on his next polite sip of horrible scotch.

"Miss Meredith," he chided once he recovered his composure, "you really do have a very singular way of expressing yourself."

Wiping his mouth with a spotless white handkerchief, he continued, "However, Mr. Calderwood is incorrect, you can take me at my word, at least as far as my intention not to harm you is concerned. All I want is for him to honour his commitment to me, you are merely a minor inconvenience and I have no wish to add further complications to what has already become a most inconvenient day."

"How dare you speak of honour, sir," Calderwood's furious voice crackled from the speaker on the phone, *"when you hold my family as hostages like a common criminal."*

"Marvin, Marvin," said Forrester, in a conciliatory tone, "you must calm yourself, I have no need to hold your tiresome relatives any longer," he smiled again at Hannah, "after all, we now have the pleasure of Miss Meredith's company."

"She has nothing to do with this, Forrester, you cannot force her to take part in your plan."

"Oh I didn't want her involved, in fact, if it wasn't for your meddling she wouldn't be here at all." He looked at Hannah, "How did you get the device to Miss Meredith anyway?"

"It's Ms. actually," feeling as if she should contribute something to proceedings, "and he didn't get anything to me, I bought it at the auction, you know that. You tried to buy it from me."

"Yes, but how did you manage it, Marvin?" Glaring at the phone, "We knew it was to be auctioned, there were a lot of other people who were expecting to see the chest it was hidden in to come up for sale. The man who won the bid was very disappointed. I believe it was his men who came after you last night, Ms. Meredith."

"Ha! You think you're so clever don't you, Forrester?" Marvin sounded positively delighted. *"But you didn't know that I'd returned to the future and moved the device when I discovered what you were planning to do with it. I hid it amongst the miscellaneous items from my workshop, in the hope you and your elitist cronies would think it unworthy of your time. It appears I was correct in my assumption, my only regret is having involved the young lady in all this."*

"Well I'm afraid she is involved, whether you like it or not, so I suggest you do as you were instructed and make the purchases we asked for," the humour was gone from Forrester's voice now, his icy gaze fixed on Hannah as he spoke, "otherwise I might be forced to change my mind about certain... rules of engagement."

"Hang on a minute, Mr. Forrester," Hannah demanded, "don't I get any say in the matter? If you're going to use me as collateral for your odious little scheme, the least you can do is consult me."

"Really?" Forrester looked surprised, "and what exactly do you think you could contribute to the discussion, Hannah... you don't mind if I call you Hannah do you, if we're going to be working together?"

"If you must," she replied coldly, "not that it appears I have any choice. But don't think for a minute I'm going to work with you. Marvin has told me what you're planning and I think you and your gang of thugs are the worst kind of scum. You do realize your greed is going to ruin entire countries and destroy the lives of millions of innocent people, don't you?"

"Oh Hannah, don't be so naïve, there are no longer any such things as *innocent people*, everyone is complicit in the ruination of society. We are just going to take it to its natural conclusion slightly earlier than would have ordinarily been the case. When we eventually take control of the shattered economy, you will see how grateful the great unwashed populace will be for some strong leadership."

"That's all very well," said Hannah, "but it isn't going to save all the businesses that collapse, or the families who won't be able to afford to pay their bills in the meantime, will it?"

"All the better for us," Forrester spoke in a matter of fact tone, as if he was talking about some sort of intellectual exercise, instead of the fall of global economic civilization "the more desperate the world gets, the more open to persuasion its governments will be when we offer them our solution."

Hannah just stared at him, the revulsion clear on her face. "You really are a psychopath, Paul," she spat out the name as if having to speak it was distasteful to her, "you don't give a shit about anyone but yourself do you?"

"On the contrary, Hannah, my only wish is to wrest power from those who have made such a mess of the world and bring it back from the brink of destruction."

"Oh you're such a philanthropist," she was about to give the smug bastard a piece of her mind when a thought occurred to her, "and I'd love to sit and listen to some more of your egomaniac power fantasies, but if I do I'm afraid I might wet myself. Am I permitted to go to the toilet?"

Forrester searched her face, seemingly for the answer to some internal question. He glanced at the front door, thought for a moment, then apparently came to a decision. "Where is it?" he asked, "I don't want you making my life difficult again."

"Past the kitchen, as you turn to the left, it's the only door."

He looked in the direction she had indicated, then stood up and walked over to the chair where his coat was hanging. He reached into the pocket and as he withdrew his hand Hannah caught her breath; he was holding a small automatic pistol.

"Oh charming, I'm to pee at gunpoint now am I?"

"Really, Hannah, you have such a low opinion of me, I'm shocked." he laughed, "No, just a precaution, I assure you. You can never be too careful."

He moved toward the doorway of the kitchen, glancing inside then looked back at Hannah, "You be a good girl and sit there a minute."

Forrester walked down the short hallway, his back against the right hand wall to give him the best view to the left. As he reached the corner he saw it was only a few paces to a closed wooden door and looked behind him into the living room.

"Are you behaving yourselves in there?" he called out. The room was L-shaped and she was sitting out of his line of sight.

"I'm not going anywhere," Hannah answered, "you've got your goons outside anyway, where would I go?"

"I do have a man stationed outside the door, yes, so it wouldn't do you any good to attempt an escape that way and I intend to make sure you can't flee from here, either."

Forrester stepped forward and opened the door, revealing a small bathroom containing just one tiny, sealed window above the bath, with an extractor fan encased in it. Behind the door, he found a toilet and a small sink with cupboards underneath. He tucked the gun into the back of his waistband and checked the cupboards, found nothing suspicious or hazardous to his well-being, walked out of the bathroom, leaving the door open behind him and headed back into the living room, again keeping to the right so he could see around the angle of the hallway before he entered the main room where Hannah sat.

As soon as Forrester was out of sight in the hallway, Hannah had stood up and grabbed the timephone, bending to unplug the adapter from the wall and placing the whole strange contraption back into the empty box.

With her heart pounding, she slipped the flick knife that she'd taken from the noseless goon out of her pocket and quietly opened it, then almost dropped it in shock when Forrester called to her from the hall. She was terrified her voice would give her away, but he seemed content with her answer and a few seconds later she heard him open the bathroom door.

Gathering her courage, she silently crept across the room as quickly as she dared, stopped just inside the kitchen doorway and waited. She heard Forrester checking the bathroom cabinets, then the sound of his footsteps coming down the hall.

She nearly cried out in surprise when he appeared, he was so close, hugging the wall and facing away from her as she had hoped. When he stepped into the main room and realized she wasn't sitting on the sofa anymore he began to turn his head.

Hannah stepped forward and brought her right hand, holding the razor sharp knife, up and around, stopped only an inch from Forrester's throat and shouted directly into his ear "DROP THE FUCKING GUN! NOW!"

Forrester froze, then slowly raised his hands to show they were empty, which was when Hannah registered the hard shape digging into her stomach and looked down.

There was a sharp intake of breath from her former captor and she realized that while she hadn't been paying attention she had nicked him with the blade. "Stand still if you want to keep breathing through the same hole you're used to," rather pleased with her first try at tough talk, "I won't tell you twice, you pompous arsehole."

He swallowed convulsively and swiveled his eyes in an attempt to see around his own head, but other than that remained silent.

Hannah yanked the pistol from his waistband with her left hand, taking some sadistic satisfaction from hearing him gasp as it scraped up his spine, withdrawing the knife at the same time as pushing him away from her with the barrel of the gun.

Then she had a stroke of luck.

He tripped on the edge of the heavy hearth rug and fell forward, throwing his raised arms out in front of him just too late to prevent him from crashing face-first into the oak mantle over the fire.

Forrester collapsed in the fireplace, bleeding from a nasty wound to the temple, and lay still.

Hannah stood, breathing heavily for a moment, before shaking herself free of the encroaching feeling of panic and quickly bent to check the motionless man's pulse.

He wasn't dead, but was all she could tell. And she honestly couldn't bring herself to care much about it either way, so she rolled him into a loose approximation of the recovery position and stood up.

Grabbing the box marked Stuff from the table, she went to the front door and looked through the peephole. Sure enough, the obedient goon was standing right in front of the door, the back of his broad neck level with Hannah's view. She saw no sign of anyone else and could just make out a darkened car parked next to her Porsche.

She counted to three and then opened the door as fast as she could.

The thug started to turn, but Hannah jabbed the pistol into the short muscly mass of his neck and he stopped.

She couldn't think of anything suitably pithy to say this time, however, so she took another deep breath, screwed her eyes up tight and brought the butt of the gun down in a rapid chopping motion on top of his head.

This didn't have quite the effect she had hoped for; the man screamed in pain and grabbed his head with both hands, so Hannah simply shoved him in the small of the back with all her strength and watched him pitch headlong down the stone steps, considerably faster than she intended. He landed at the bottom in an untidy heap, his neck at an angle that didn't bode well for his future good health.

Hannah didn't bother to check him as she hurried down the steps, she suspected there was no point, and made for the cars. Hardly even hesitating, she shot out both the tyres on one side of the black BMW, before climbing into her car, dumping the box, containing the only link to the one person who could help her, onto the passenger seat beside her and slammed the door.

As she swung the Porsche round in front of the cottage where she had spent so many relaxing weekends, and accelerated up the bumpy track in the first grey light of morning, she congratulated herself on her escape, against all the odds, made a mental note to have a massive nervous breakdown whenever the opportunity presented itself, and tried to think what to do next.

10
Anger and Allies

Hannah skidded to a halt at the top of the track that led to Black's Lodge, paused to consider her limited options and swung the Porsche to the left, onto the main road, heading towards a glow in the sky that marked the dawning of another day in her increasingly confusing life.

Realizing she was trembling and gripping the wheel with a painful ferocity, she made a conscious effort to relax, rolling her shoulders and taking a series of long, slow breaths, forcing herself to calm down. After a few minutes, she managed to get the shakes under control and tried to focus on what her next move should be.

Hannah knew one thing for sure; she was bloody furious.

For now, her anger was directed, not at the unseen cause of her predicament, Marvin Calderwood, but at Paul Forrester and his cohorts. How could they be so callous, so blind to the catastrophic effects of the plan they were hoping to execute?

They were insane, that was the only explanation, the greed and thirst for power had driven them over the edge. That, or it was just Forrester who was insane, and had kept his megalomaniacal tendencies a secret from his co-conspirators. Simply using them for their resources to assist him in his bid for world domination until it was too late for them to see what they'd got themselves into. Either way, she was damned if she was going to stand by and let the arrogant bastards get away with it, especially while she still had the means to stop them.

She glanced at the box on the passenger seat, now

rather battered and torn, the word Stuff just visible on one side, and wondered what Marvin must be thinking right now. Well, not "right now" exactly, but Hannah had decided early on that trying to think in too many tenses at once made her head hurt. It was vital for her to find somewhere private to plug the phone in to talk to him and let him know she was ok, and see if he had any helpful suggestions on the subject.

Hannah was surprised there was so little traffic around, even at this time in the morning, until it dawned on her it was Saturday. She was still wondering whether this was a good or bad thing when something poked her in the subconscious. She slammed on the brakes and backed up so she could read the sign she had just passed.

"Calderwood Middle School," she read out loud and laughed, "Well, if that isn't a good omen then I don't know what is."

Checking to make sure she was unobserved, Hannah drove down the tree-lined slope that led to a large, red brick Victorian building. She followed signs around the school itself, out of view from the road, and found a parking area overlooking playing fields and dense woodland beyond. The car park was empty and she parked as close to the main building as she could, grabbing the box as she got out of the car.

She stood for a moment, listening for sounds of life, and when she was satisfied she was alone, Hannah made for the nearest window and peered into the dim interior of a large classroom with no phone in sight. She moved further along the wall until she turned a corner and found a series of windows looking into a long corridor opening up into some sort of reception area.

"Ah, this looks more like it."

Putting the box down Hannah took Forrester's pistol from her pocket, checked to make sure the safety catch was securely engaged before holding it by the barrel and used the stock that had been so ineffective at breaking skulls, to smash one of the old metal-framed windows so she could reach through and release the catch.

Placing the box just inside the window she heaved herself up and over the ledge, dangling in the uncomfortable position of being half-in, half-out, with her stomach taking all her weight. She twisted awkwardly to reach the box and lowered it to the floor of the corridor, then joined it in an undignified heap as she slithered the rest of the way through the window. Picking up the box, Hannah made for the large wooden reception desk, peering carefully into the lobby first to make sure nobody was around.

Sure enough, there was a large switchboard telephone console on the desk and Hannah traced the cable to a recessed socket on the floor. She unplugged the cable and was attaching the timephone adapter when a voice behind her nearly gave her a heart attack.

"Good morning Ms. Meredith, I hope your weekend is going well so far."

Hannah spun around, her hand instinctively going to the pocket holding the gun, bringing her face to face for the second time, and at least two times too many as far as she was concerned, with Bronk, the peculiar looking man she'd last seen at that bloody auction. "What the *fuck* are you doing here?"

She literally could not believe her eyes. "How the... how did you..?" she stopped, her eyes widening and her hand, finally obeying the instruction her brain had been frantically sending it for the last five seconds, yanked the gun out of her pocket and pointed it in a suitably dramatic, double-handed grip at Bronk's grinning face, which was spoiled only slightly when she had to fumble around to check the safety was off.

"You're with that bastard Forrester aren't you?" She looked past him down the corridor, expecting to see hordes of heavily armed, madly-grinning assassins swarming towards her. Come to think of it, why were so many people grinning at her recently? Nothing even remotely amusing had happened as far as she could see, quite the contrary in fact. Maybe it was her sense of humour, she sometimes missed the subtleties but, apart from the now considerably less-amused looking Bronk, the school still appeared quiet.

"I assure you…" began the strange little man, but Hannah cut him off.

"Don't you "I assure you" me!" she snapped, frowning slightly as she replayed the words to herself, then continued, rather lamely, "by which I mean, don't assure me of anything, unless it's something I want to hear..um..and unless it's the truth, I mean, obviously."

She stared at Bronk's terrified expression and decided he was no immediate threat. "I'm already having a bad day, I haven't slept and I'm very on edge. It wouldn't take much for there to be a nasty shooting accident, is what I'm saying, due to an unfortunate misunderstanding and nervous exhaustion."

"I assu…" Bronk stopped, looking at the gun and flinching, "I give you my word that I have no affiliation with Mr. Forrester. In fact, I'm here to help you, since it is partly my fault that you currently find yourself a target for his particular form of unhinged egomania." He flinched again when he saw the look on Hannah's face.

"What do you mean, it's your fault?" Hannah glared at him, "What do you have to do with all this if you're not working for Forrester?"

"It was a terrible mistake, I can only apologise," seeing her expression he hurried on, "I spotted you in the bar before the auction and genuinely believed you to be one of the invited guests, it was the only reason you were admitted. The start of the Calderwood sale was to be a separate, private affair, the main auction was to follow after the first few lots were sold."

Hannah kept the gun trained on Bronk's sweating face and asked, "So, it was purely by chance that I was the only one there who didn't know what the rest of them were there to bid for, and purely by chance that I ended up with that box?" Before he could answer, another thought occurred to her, "Did you even know what was in the box?"

"Oh yes, I knew what was in there alright," Bronk grinned again, despite the gun, "but they didn't know that I knew, that's the important thing. They had no idea the chronophonic device had been moved, no idea that I had discovered it when I was sorting through sale items for the auction, and they had no interest in the miscellany of a life's scientific innovation, they only cared about acquiring the way to fulfill their dreams of power and they all thought that was in Marvin's fancy chest..."

"Hang on," Hannah interrupted him again, "you called it a *"chronophonic device"* and you say all this as if you knew about Marvin and his discovery." Hannah, warily lowered the gun and motioned Bronk to the chair behind the desk, "what are you not telling me? Don't try anything, I'm watching you."

Bronk sat down and looked up at her in surprise. "Know about him?" he said with a dry laugh, "Why, I should say I know about him, I was assistant for nearly five years."

11
Reunions and Revelations

Hannah Hannah stared at Bronk, her mouth open in shock. "His assistant? You? So Forrester is after you too, he must be."

"No, I'm happy to say that he knows, or at least knew, nothing of my involvement, although my absence may now have been noticed by one of his thugs, I had to borrow one of their cars to follow you," he gestured to the right hand pocket of the shapeless black overcoat he wore, "may I?"

"You may not!" Hannah raised the hand holding the gun, "What's in there anyway?"

"I thought you might be hungry," said Bronk with a wry smile, "I'm guessing you didn't have time for breakfast, or dinner last night, for that matter."

At the thought of food, Hannah's stomach gave a loud growl and Bronk laughed. "It sounds like that's a "yes" then?"

"Slowly," she warned him, "with your left hand."

"A very wise precaution, Ms. Meredith, but I promise you, I mean you no harm."

Bronk reached awkwardly across his body and reached into the pocket, all the while keeping his eyes fixed on Hannah, bringing out a paper bag, held between finger and thumb, which he laid on the reception desk and sat back in his chair.

"After you," said Hannah, "let's see what's on the menu."

"Oh, really, you still don't trust me?" he shrugged, "That's ok, you've no reason to, I suppose."

He leaned forward and carefully ripped the edge of the bag, which had a baker's logo printed on the front, opening it up to reveal two large Danish pastries, causing Hannah's stomach to make another audible protest. Bronk tore a small chunk from each pastry and ate them one after the other.

"There, happy now?" he asked, raising a quizzical eyebrow.

Hannah hesitated for about two seconds, then grabbed the nearest Danish and bit off a huge mouthful. "Sod it, at least I won't die hungry." She swallowed, paused, apparently decided she hadn't been poisoned and made short work of the rest of it.

Bronk sat in silence, a look of amusement on his face, until she finished eating, then reached over and pushed the remaining pastry towards her.

"You don't want it?" Hannah asked.

"I already ate," replied Bronk, "besides, I reckon you need all the energy you can get, you've had a rough night, from what I can tell." He nodded down at his other pocket, "I have coffee. A flask in my coat."

"Coffee? I might be starting to like you, Mr. Bronk."

Hannah motioned to him and he slipped off his coat and hung it over the chair, pulling a plastic Thermos from his pocket and placing it on the desk. He unscrewed the lid and poured steaming black coffee into it. "It's Bronk, Ms. Meredith, just Bronk is fine."

She picked up the coffee and smelled it, the rich aroma alone making her feel better. She took a sip and studied the man in front of her. "Ok then, and I suppose you had better call me Hannah. But only on the condition that you tell me how the hell you found me and how you managed to stay off Forrester's radar."

Bronk looked at his watch, glanced out at the grey morning beyond the windows, then back at Hannah. "Alright, I think we're safe enough for now, but we'll need to talk to Marvin before too long." He lowered his head, seeming to collect his thoughts for a few moments, then began to talk in a calm measured voice. "I'd been working with Marvin in his workshop, helping him perfect the design for his steam turbine, when he received a call from the government, asking for his help on a secret project…"

Bronk went on to confirm the story Marvin Calderwood told her earlier, including the discovery of the wormhole, created by the giant generators, but at this point, his story diverged from Marvin's version of events.

"…we were taking readings at the edge of the rift when I thought I saw movement on the other side," Bronk shook his head, remembering, "I reached out for it without thinking, a reflex, nothing more, but that was all it took. The next thing I knew, I was lying in the garden of a large house on the outskirts of London," he looked straight into Hannah's eyes, "in 1976!"

"But that's the same year Marvin arrived," said Hannah, "did he follow you, then? I still don't understand why he never told me about you, you must have both been here at the same time." She was having trouble getting her head around this time travel business and the fact that Calderwood hadn't mentioned Bronk made her suspicious.

"Unfortunately, it doesn't seem to work like that," Bronk grimaced, "it appears it was several weeks before Marvin worked out that I'd been drawn through the rift and when he followed, this end of the rift had moved, in space if not in time, and he found himself here, many miles away from where I ended up. So even if we arrived at the exact same minute, despite leaving our own time weeks apart, we would not have known about it."

Bronk went on to relate a similar tale of disorientation and dislocation to the one she'd heard from Marvin, this one with a less dramatic ending, but no less astonishing for all that.

Bronk had also used his engineering skills to make a

living in the unfamiliar future world he had been stranded in, traveling around doing mechanical repairs and casual labour until he'd landed a job with the auction house, assessing specialty equipment for the owners, helping them to determine its resale value. It was this piece of luck, coincidence, fate, call it what you will, which first brought him into contact with members of the mysterious cabal, revealing the millionaire businessmen's obsession with finding Marvin's device.

"When I realised the estate I'd been sent to assess was that of Marvin Calderwood, I couldn't believe my luck," Bronk laughed at the memory, "and that's where I met Paul Forrester for the first time. He was perfectly charming to start with. Then, when he couldn't find what he wanted at the auction, I saw his true face and it isn't something I want to experience again any time soon. He was furious, screaming that he'd been cheated and ranting about traitors in his inner circle, it was frightening."

Hannah watched Bronk as he told his story and had to admit that he was pretty convincing. "So," she concluded, "say I believe you, how are you going to help me? It sounds as though you're just as likely to be on Forrester's shit-list as I am."

"I know how to replicate the generator Marvin designed, which would again anchor the rift in one place, enabling us to travel back and forth in safety, even allowing us to bring Marvin back to the here and now with us, should he wish to return, but I need to speak to him first."

"I was about to contact him when you arrived with breakfast," swigging the cold remains of her coffee and nodding at the timephone with its trailing cable, "it should plug into that floor socket, now it has the adapter attached to it."

Bronk bent down and clicked the adapter into the phone socket, plugged the switchboard unit back in and turned on Marvin's extraordinary device. They listened to the metallic hiss for what seemed like ages, then, *"Hello? ...hello, is that you, Hannah?"*

"Hello Marvin, I'm here," Hannah was surprisingly relieved to hear his voice again, after all the trouble he'd caused her, "and I have someone who is very keen to speak to you."

"Oh my dear young lady, I'm so glad you are safe. Did you escape from the clutches of that evil monster, Forrester, or does he have you calling me under duress?"

"I'm fine, although I think your friend Paul may have a bit of a headache this morning. No, I think you'll be surprised when I tell you who I've been having breakfast with today." She looked at Bronk, shrugged and poured herself the last of the coffee, "I'll hand you over."

"Good morning Marvin, or maybe it's afternoon there now," said Bronk, grinning up at Hannah, "depending on whether you ever got those magnetic field dampers working properly…"

"What?...wait, who is that? Bronk, is that you?" Marvin sounded like he was going to faint. *"But, but, you... you vanished!"*

"I'm sorry Marvin, it's a rather long story and we are somewhat pressed for time, I'll explain later. But for now, we need your advice."

12
Making Plans

Bronk spoke to Marvin in a respectful but forceful voice and Hannah couldn't help noticing the marked difference between the man she'd just eaten breakfast with and the wheedling, obsequious little man she had first met the night before, at the auction. Bloody hell, she thought to herself, how did my life manage to get so out of control in less than 24 hours?

He seemed to have more of a presence about him now, as if he'd somehow been hiding himself away behind a facade and Hannah was only now seeing him as he truly was.

"Marvin, listen," said Bronk, glancing again at his watch, "I need to know whether you found a way to stabilize the portal entrance and pin it down to a specific geographical location. Do we need to build a generator to anchor it at this end?"

"Hannah, are you there?" It was as though Marvin Calderwood hadn't even heard Bronk. *"Hannah? Ms. Meredith? Are you absolutely sure this man is who he says he is?"*

"As sure as I can be," Hannah replied, "which, I might add, is about as sure as I can be of anything at the moment. He did keep the timephone safe after you moved it, and made sure it didn't come to the attention of Forrester and his goons. He could easily have stolen it himself if he'd wanted to, but it seems as though he's just been monitoring my progress since I fell down the rabbit hole last night," Hannah scowled at Bronk, "although he didn't see fit to offer his assistance at any point."

"In my defense," Bronk cut in before Marvin could interrupt, "I was heavily outnumbered at Ms. Meredith's house and, as for Forrester and his bodyguard at the cottage, I thought Hannah handled herself admirably. She even shot out the tyres on his car, did you know that?" he grinned up at Hannah, "I would have been ready if she'd needed help, but my services were not required."

"It still would have been nice to know I had back-up," Hannah grumbled, "if I'd seen you, I might have shot you too, I did think you were working for them at the time, remember?"

"I can only apologise once again," Bronk remarked, "but right now we have more important things to attend to and I'm starting to tire of explaining myself. So Marvin, if you're satisfied that I'm not an imposter, would you please answer my question, how do we overcome the instability of the portal entrance?"

"Very well," Marvin appeared mollified, at least for now, on the question of Bronk's identity. *"I will take you at your word and I suspect Hannah would not be so easily fooled."* He paused and they heard what sounded like a heavy sigh over the echoing connection.

"I'm very glad you are safe, Bronk, I was sure you had perished, torn apart by the rift."

"No, I assume my journey through the portal was much the same as yours. Instantaneous and, barring a headache and a terrible thirst when I arrived, without incident or injury of any kind," Bronk looked nervously out of the window, checking they remained undiscovered in the deserted school, "but what I could never work out was why we came out at two separate locations."

"I think I may have the answer to your question," Marvin answered, *"although I didn't find out until it was too late. It wasn't until I returned there, to my future, that I realized something was wrong. Because, like you, I didn't arrive in the same location as I did the first time. I*

was expecting to appear in my private laboratory, from whence I had originally traveled back into the past, but I was nearly seventy miles away and it took me all night to get home, never mind the fright I gave to the congregation of the church in which I materialized, I swear they thought I was the Second Coming."

Marvin laughed at the memory, but Bronk was getting impatient and Hannah could see he was tired of listening to his old mentor's reminiscences, so she tried to nudge Marvin back on track. "I expect you, being a clever chap like you are, worked out why you came out somewhere different eventually though, didn't you?"

"As I said, it wasn't until after I returned home the second time, it occurred to me that maybe the portal wasn't actually moving at all. Maybe it was us who had moved instead."

"What do you mean, we moved?" Bronk sounded interested, despite himself.

"What if the portal was fixed at this end, in both time and space, but only fixed in time at the end that exits to the future?"

Hannah screwed up her forehead in concentration, trying to get her brain to accept these outlandish concepts. "I don't get it," she admitted, "why wouldn't it be the same at each end?"

"I think what Marvin is saying, in his usual, roundabout way, is at his end of the wormhole it is dependent on the generator for its very existence, therefore it only exists at that point in time and space." He looked at Hannah, who nodded, although not all that certain, "At this end, there is nothing to anchor it to a definitive point, so it only stays steady at the same point in time, not space."

"Even that isn't quite right," chimed in Marvin's tinny voice from the phone speaker, sounding rather smug, Hannah thought, *"because it would be more accurate to say that it is in the same point in space, but not the same*

point in geography."

"What d'you..?" began Bronk, but before he could finish, Hannah interrupted him.

"Rotation!" she suddenly burst out, to a look of confused irritation on Bronk's face, "The Earth is rotating, isn't it? The point on the ground where the portal appears is rolling around underneath it! Is that what you mean by "geography" Marvin?"

Marvin Calderwood laughed in surprise. *"Very good, Hannah, you've got it exactly! That's precisely the reason that Bronk and I arrived so far apart, despite entering your timeline at the same exact moment. Although we arrived at the same time, we left several weeks apart. By the time I followed Bronk through the rift, The Earth's rotation had moved the ground "under" the portal, for want of a better word, so I was deposited in a correspondingly distant location."*

"So we're no nearer finding a way to bring you back here," said Hannah, "this has all been for nothing."

"But what good would that do?" Marvin asked. *"What could I do if I returned there? Forrester now has control of my equipment and the laboratory that contains the generator, so even if I did return, the only place I could be sure of ending up would be right at the centre of his web. And that's only assuming someone could get to the generator to operate it, otherwise, we would have the same problem. No way of anchoring the wormhole, and no way of telling where I'd arrive."*

"But if you were here, now," said Bronk, "you wouldn't be there, then, to help Paul Forrester carry out his plan. Don't you understand? Without somebody to blackmail into buying up the controlling interests in all those young, growing businesses for him; the ones that will eventually go on to make Forrester and his cronies fabulously wealthy and give them their power base, he won't have the resources available to stage his insane scheme for a global financial coups d'état."

There was silence for a moment as they absorbed this, then Hannah frowned and asked, "I've no idea how all this stuff works, obviously, but surely the Earth goes round at a constant speed," she looked at Bronk, "doesn't it?"

"Yes, of course, but…"

"Then can't you just look at a map and work out which bit is going to be under the wormhole at the time Marvin comes through?"

"It's not as simple as that," said Bronk, "without a generator to anchor this end in the present, Marvin will arrive in 1976, where the wormhole originally came out when we discovered it. It's only with the power of the generator that we can divert its course, so that it will terminate in our present day, instead of forty years ago."

"Wait!" The shout made Hannah jump. *"Wait, there is a way!"*

They could hear the excitement in Marvin's voice. *"My God, why didn't I think of it earlier? Once a connection is established through the chronophonic device, it should give a stable enough signal for me to detect from this end. I will then be able to recalibrate the generator to use that signal for an anchor point."*

"So you could come here right now?" asked Hannah.

"No, unfortunately, it won't be powerful enough to also produce a geographical anchor, so you'll need to already be in the correct location before you activate the device."

"And you can work that out, knowing the speed of rotation?" Hannah looked at Bronk, who had been following the exchange with intense concentration.

"Yes, it's a fairly simple equation," he replied, "we may need to factor for precession but…"

"Don't get all technical on me," said Hannah with a frown, "just a simple yes would have done."

"Marvin," Bronk said, "I need you to tell me precisely

when and where you last came through the rift, I have to have a starting point for my calculations…"

Hannah excused herself while they talked scientific gobbledygook to each other and went in search of a toilet. All that coffee had finally kick-started her metabolism and she needed to freshen up.

Ten minutes later and already feeling better, she was walking back towards the reception area, looking through the window which overlooked the playing fields behind the school, when she thought she noticed movement in the treeline of the distant woodland. She stopped and shielded her eyes against the watery sun that was finally putting in an appearance.

There! She was sure now, somebody was making their way, as stealthily as they could along the border of the woods, heading for the corner where the field met the school building. Hannah turned and hurried back, to find Bronk packing the timephone into its battered cardboard box.

He looked up as she entered the lobby, raising his eyebrows in silent inquiry.

"We have to go," said Hannah, "we've got company."

13
Taking Control

"Shouldn't we call the Boss, tell 'im we found 'er?" Frank asked uncertainly, squinting up at the hulking shape of Toby, his goon-superior, silhouetted against the hazy glare of the morning sun.

"No, Frank," he replied with a weary sigh, "that's exactly what we don't do. Remember what happened to Alvin when he got all cocky at that bitch's house? He called the Boss before he made sure they had her, told him it was all sorted didn't he? Now, where's Alvin? Bottom of a flooded quarry somewhere, that's where. No fingertips, and a splintered mess where his teeth used to be, most likely."

Toby shaded his eyes and peered across the playing fields towards the school, "No, we make bloody sure we've got her before we call anyone, I'm too attached to my extremities, thank you very much."

They'd been following the bitch since she'd left her house, using the tracker Forrester had attached to her fancy car. Lucky for him, since he'd lost her at the lake.

Toby and Frank had trekked through the fucking woods in the early morning mist, to come out behind the deserted school, when they got a call saying the signal had stopped moving. Frank had done nothing but moan and fucking complain since they'd left the car on the other side of the tangled, overgrown woodland and fought their way through half a mile of brambles and grasping creepers, finally arriving here on the edge of the field where they had been crouched in the damp grass for the last ten minutes.

Toby had a nasty gash across his forehead from a branch Frank had whipped into his face, there was a long rip in the shoulder of Frank's suit jacket and Toby's handmade Italian shoes were completely ruined, so neither of them were in the best of moods.

"We'll find out where she is and surprise her," said Toby, "she won't know what's hit her. You still got that taser?"

Frank patted his jacket pocket and nodded.

"Good. The Boss doesn't want her harmed. Not too badly anyway," he grinned maliciously, "but you can still give her fucking good belt with that and she'll be fine later."

Frank pulled out the taser pistol, checked the charge and shrugged. "I'm easy either way, I'll 'appily kill the evil cow, I fink she's got it coming for what she did to Rory with that poker, poor bastard."

"Just do as you're fucking told and we'll be fine," snapped Toby irritably, "be a good boy and leave the thinking to me, ok?"

Frank scowled, grumbled under his breath and shoved the taser back into his pocket.

Then the two grumpy, disheveled thugs carefully picked their way along the tree line until they reached the back of the main building. Toby edged around the corner and made his way along the wall, taking care not to raise his head above the level of the windows. Suddenly he stopped and Frank bumped into him with a curse, when he felt a crunch under the sole of his once-beautiful shoe. He looked down and saw shards of broken glass on the path, then looked up and smiled with satisfaction.

"Now we've got you, bitch." Toby hissed, pointing upward and making sure Frank saw the window Hannah had smashed earlier.

Frank nodded and looked around for something to climb on, then he realized Toby was staring at him impatiently, his hands clasped together in front of him.

Frank glanced once more up at the window, reached for the sill, planted his foot in Toby's hands and heaved himself up until he could see into the corridor. He listened, but couldn't detect any sounds from inside, so he clambered through and stood silently for a moment. When he was sure nobody had noticed his arrival, he leaned out of the window and signaled Toby he was going to investigate. Toby gave him the ok, tapped his watch and held up his hand, fingers spread; five minutes. Frank nodded and pulled out the taser as he cautiously crept toward the lobby.

"We have to go," Hannah announced, "we've got company."

"What do you mean company, who is it?" asked Bronk.

"I'm not sure, but anyone skulking around in the woods in a suit at this time in the morning is up to no good as far as I'm concerned," she replied, "come and have a look."

Bronk grabbed the box and followed her along the corridor to where she was looking out across the playing fields and scanned the distant line of trees.

"There they are," Hannah pointed, "you see them, kneeling down by the fence, there's two of them?" He watched, then nodded thoughtfully.

"Uh-oh, they're on the move," She ducked back behind the wall and looked at Bronk, "what should we do?"

"Well, it can't be a coincidence that they just popped out of the woods right there, which means they must have already known you were here." Bronk risked a quick look out the window and his gaze fell on Hannah's Porsche, "They couldn't have somehow traced your car could they?"

"Of course!" Hannah could have kicked herself, "They probably stuck a bug on it, that would explain how they found me at the lake house. Damn, I should have guessed."

"Never mind that," said Bronk, smiling "because now we have the advantage. We know they're here and, despite the fact they know you are here, they don't know about me and they don't know, we know, they're here."

"Do you have to talk in riddles all the time," snapped Hannah, "this whole thing is confusing enough as it is."

"My apologies, but the fact remains, we have to use the element of surprise while we have it, especially when they think it's theirs."

"So what can we do?" Hannah looked around the empty corridor, "it's not like we're spoilt for the choice of weapons."

"Oh, I'm sure we can find something." Bronk turned and walked back until he reached the bank of signs on the wall, looked down it for a few seconds and then beckoned Hannah to follow him.

They crossed the reception area and took a left turn, walking up to a set of double doors marked Sports Hall. Bronk pushed through the doors and they stepped into the large open space beyond.

The hall was obviously used for several activities, with exercise equipment, small goalposts, and basketball hoops at one end and long nets hanging from the ceiling at the other, forming an enclosed area for cricket practice, where batsman could safely clout balls around to their hearts' content, without risk of injuring fellow sportsmen.

Hannah picked up a cricket bat, testing the weight and swing of it in her hand, "Well it's not exactly a light sabre, but it'll certainly give someone a nasty headache."

But Bronk didn't seem to be listening, he was looking at a piece of equipment Hannah hadn't noticed at first, it looked like some sort of telescope to her, or maybe a camera; a complicated looking tube shaped device on a tripod with a plastic box on top of it.

Bronk turned to her with a grin, "I think I might have an idea…"

Frank had reached the lobby without incident, looked around for signs of recent activity and after finding the remains of Hannah's breakfast on the desk, located a fire door to the rear of the building and let Toby in.

Frank showed him the half eaten pastry and flask and was about to ask what they should do next when they both heard a noise coming from down the corridor.

Hannah stood on the left hand side just inside the double doors, clutching the cricket bat in both hands, wearing a protective helmet with a sturdy wire guard across her face and heavy batsman's gloves.

Bronk stood twenty feet away, behind the tripod mounted device, which was positioned so that it faced the centre of the doorway.

Hannah heard the fire exit closing down the corridor and looked at Bronk.

He paused, then nodded to her.

Swallowing nervously, Hannah reached forward with her bat and pushed over the rack of hockey sticks she'd dragged over to the doorway, wincing as they hit the wooden floor with an almighty crash. She immediately took up position again, back against the wall, bat raised like a battle club, eyes fixed on the doors.

"What was that?" Toby asked. "It came from down there," pointing down the short corridor ahead of them, "quick, the bitch may be trying to escape."

They hurried to the set of doors and waited, listening.

Frank looked at Toby, pointed a stubby finger at himself, then at the door, took a firm grip on the taser with one hand and grabbed the right hand door handle with the other.

Toby took hold of the other handle and nodded to Frank. He counted down; three, two, one on his fingers and then threw the door open.

Frank did the same, taking two rapid steps into the hall with the stun gun held at arm's length and then stopping in confusion.

He said, "You? But..." when he recognized Bronk behind the strange contraption in the middle of the floor. Then there was a whirring noise and a hollow pop, like a cork being expelled from a very large bottle.

Frank had a brief second to register the cricket ball, traveling towards him at roughly sixty miles an hour from the barrel of the bowling machine, before it struck him in the centre of his ribcage.

The hand not holding the taser grabbed at his chest, just in time for two things to happen at once; the second ball was flung from the mouth of the deadly accurate tube, hitting the exact same spot and breaking Frank's clutching fingers as he desperately tried to catch his breath and Hannah stepped forward and brought the cricket bat down on his forearm, causing him to drop the pistol with a furious bellow.

Hannah swung round to face the door, just in time to see Toby duck the third ball as it shot out of the hall and bounced down the corridor. She bent to pick up the taser, pointed it at him from a distance of only a few feet and said, "I expect you have all sorts of nasty little ideas about what you'd like to do now, haven't you? Well, unless you want to be lit up like a Christmas tree, just don't!"

14
And then there were three

Keeping low to avoid the steady stream of cricket balls Bronk was cheerfully feeding into the machine, Toby looked up at Hannah, who was glaring at him through the wire visor of her helmet, the taser pointed unwaveringly at his chest.

We can't let the bitch escape now, he thought, not when we've got her cornered. He glanced over at Frank, on his knees and still clutching his broken fingers to his chest, making nasty wheezy, gasping noises. Ok, Toby thought, maybe not we, but I'll be fucked if I'm letting her get away again.

He came to a snap decision and made a grab for the ankle holster he always wore on these unpredictable operations, which was when Hannah hit him with the taser. The charge from the stun gun's twin probes had an instant effect. The muscular spasms induced by the electric shock caused Toby to jerk upright, just in time for Bronk's final ballistic cricket ball to catch him between the eyes, snapping his head back and felling him like a rotten tree.

Hannah looked in horrified fascination from Toby's crumpled body, to the taser in her hand, to Bronk, standing behind the still whirring but empty bowling machine and back to the taser again.

"How was I to know he'd stand up like that?" Bronk said, "He shouldn't have gone for his gun, it's his own fault."

"Is… is he dead?" asked Hannah, dropping the taser, its wires still attached to Toby's motionless body, "I didn't mean to kill him," she paused, looking thoughtful, "much.

We need to talk to him, apart from anything else."

Hannah cautiously approached and kicked Toby's foot, which flopped sideways like a dead leather fish. She bent down, pulled up his torn and muddy trousers to reveal the holster strapped to his leg and removed a small pistol, which she turned and trained on Frank.

The injured goon sat on the floor and groaned in pain, his damaged hand now badly swollen and turning dark purple, his breath coming in harsh hacking coughs as he massaged his equally bruised chest and glowered furiously at the world in general.

"Now then," said Hannah, "I think it's about time we had some answers from you."

Frank just stared at her.

"I've had enough of running around like a headless chicken, at the mercy of that bunch of elitist psychos and you're going to provide us with some leverage."

This at least gave Frank something to amuse him, although his laugh was bitter and sardonic. "Ha! You don't really fink they care what 'appens to the likes of me, do you? Me and Toby, we is disposable and no mistake," he coughed again and winced, "those toffs ain't your decent criminal types, they'd sell their own gran if there was dosh to be 'ad. Bastards."

He frowned up at Bronk, as if trying to place him, then he shook his head, "You, we never even thought about you, why're you 'ere then, what's she to you?" he jerked his head in Hannah's direction, "You tryin' to nab that box 'n'all, wanna get rich quick like the rest of those fuckers do you?"

"Actually…" began Bronk.

But Frank wasn't having any of it. He spat on the floor at Bronk's feet and turned his baleful glare on Hannah. "You're all the fucking same, you nobs, got loads and you still want more, while the likes of me and Toby over there," he glanced at his fallen colleague, "we started off with fuck all an' we've still got most of it left, if you know what I mean. Well, it ain't fair and I ain't telling you nuffing."

It was no good. The stress of the day, the lack of food and sleep, the moody pooch of Frank's big, grumpy bulldog face and his sulky outburst was too much for her and Hannah burst out in a hysterical fit of the giggles. When she finally managed to compose herself, both men were gaping at her in amazement, as if they had suddenly noticed they were in a room with a crazy person and were trying to think of a safe way to escape.

"Alright, alright, there's no need to stare," said Hannah in a voice that sounded to her, like her fourth-grade schoolmistress, "for goodness sake, come on, I'm allowed a small breakdown, surely? It has been rather a long day already and it's not even lunchtime."

Bronk walked over to where Hannah was awkwardly struggling to remove the cricket helmet while trying to hold Toby's gun on Frank. "Here, let me have that," extending his hand, "I'll make sure he behaves."

Hannah rounded on him, the pistol pointing at his stomach and Bronk raised his hands and stepped back hurriedly. "Ms. Meredith, I mean Hannah, please, we've come this far, you have to trust someone sometime."

Hannah's shoulders slumped, "I'm sorry, you're right, I do trust you. It's all just been a bit... you know." she sighed in resignation, handed Bronk the gun and pried the helmet off, nearly removing her ears in the process, "Ok, so what now?"

Bronk, keeping a wary eye on Wheezy Frank, walked over to the doorway and knelt down beside Possibly Terminal Toby, felt for a pulse at his throat for a few seconds and then looked up to meet Hannah's unflinching gaze. "Nope," he shook his head, "looks like a fractured skull, I'm pretty sure a concave forehead is a bad symptom."

"Oh my God, I've killed someone else," said Hannah in a shocked voice, "I'm going to go to prison, aren't I?" Pausing to think about her situation for a second, "If I don't get killed first."

"No," said Bronk, "you didn't. And no, you're not. You defended yourself against a man who was intent on killing you. It was the cricket ball that killed him, all you did was immobilize him."

Hannah looked uncertain, then seemed to come to a decision. "I've done nothing wrong," she spoke with conviction now, "this was all brought upon me by evil, greedy men and I was simply defending myself."

She considered this for a moment, then nodded to herself and looked up. "Ok." She smiled, "I'm ok now."

Bronk looked at her, shrugged and said, "I think we should leave as quickly as possible. We will have to take our new friend with us of course," he nodded at Frank, who glared back, "are you going to come quietly, Mr…?"

"Frank, the name's Frank," he growled, "and you can fuck off, I ain't going nowhere with you two."

"Frank, Frank," said Bronk placatingly, "you've got us all wrong, we're as keen to see the toffs and nobs pay for their crimes as you are. Why do you think Forrester and his goons – no offence – have been trying to track down Ms. Meredith here, hmm?"

Frank screwed up his considerable forehead with the Herculean effort of deductive reasoning, but he apparently came up empty and just looked at Bronk, shrugged his massive shoulders and gave a non-committal grunt.

"Because she has the power to bring their entire plan crashing down around their privileged, upper-class ears, that's why. Hannah is the one person who can stop them and I'm going to help her in any way I can."

Bronk sighed and put his hand on Frank's shoulder, shaking his head sadly. "It's such a pity you're going to have to go back to Mr. Forrester and explain what happened and why you didn't capture Ms. Meredith for him."

"Oh, Toby'll do that," said Frank, with visible relief, "he's good at all that…dip-lo-macy bollocks. He's my guvnor, see? "With power comes responsibility, Frank", that's what he always tells me, and I'm happy with that, I don't want no responsibility, thank you very much."

"There is a bit of bad news on that front though, isn't there Frank? Toby isn't going to be there to help you, I'm afraid. Looks like you'll have to take some responsibility this time." Bronk sighed again and watched as a look of panic slowly clouded Frank's features.

"But there it is," he continued, "the burden of promotion, you're an important man now. If only we could afford you, we'd jump at the chance to have an experienced security specialist like yourself on our side, but I know men of your calibre don't come cheap…"

"Work for you, you mean?" Frank had seen a straw float past and was clearly tempted to grasp it, "An' you're gonna stop Forrester?"

"That's the plan Frank, yes," said Hannah, grinning at Bronk over Frank's head, "and to beat him we're going to need someone who has inside information."

"Oh that's me," said Frank, suddenly eager to please "I've got a radio in the car, maps, addresses, everything."

He grinned up at them, nursing his puffy, purple and black hand, "I even know where there's a place to hole up, me and Toby got some gear stashed there, from… undercover operations," he winked conspiratorially and tapped the side of his nose, "a place the bosses don't know about, we'll be alright there for a while, s'got a phone and all that there too."

"Congratulations Frank, you've got the job," said Bronk, offering his hand to the bemused goon. Frank beamed, enveloped Bronk's fingers in his one giant good hand and heaved himself upright.

"I do believe you just earned yourself your first bonus too," grinned Bronk, "I might even throw in lunch."

Twenty minutes later, after Frank had been with Bronk in the Porsche to show him where Toby had parked, they returned in a Range Rover and collected Hannah and her box of Stuff, the thing that had started all this madness in the first place.

"I left the keys in your car, with any luck someone will steal it and Forrester can chase some other poor buggers around the countryside for a while."

"Right," said Hannah, climbing into the back seat, "did somebody say something about lunch?"

15
Go, Team!

"This is a very flashy car, Frank," said Hannah, as Bronk pulled the Range Rover out of the school driveway and turned onto the road, "Forrester certainly looks after his goons... sorry, security consultants, doesn't he? All part of the benefits package I suppose." She smiled to herself in satisfaction as she saw Frank's jaw muscles clench, presumably biting back the sort of aggressive response that he would have to learn to control if they were to work together against their common enemy.

Frank twisted around to look at her from the front seat, wincing in pain as the movement pulled at the bruised muscles of his chest. "It was Toby's," he said with a scowl, "Toby loved this motor, Mr. Forrester gave it to 'im when 'e was promoted to team leader."

"Yes, but Toby was a company man, wasn't he?" Bronk continued, "Not an independent thinker like you, Frank."

Frank thought about this, turning to stare out of the window for a moment before replying. "S'true enough, 'e thought the sun shone out of those toff's arses, that's for sure, it did piss me off sometimes, the way 'e sucked up to 'em all the fucking time."

"That's the trouble with career climbers, you see," said Bronk, "they don't care about the ones they clamber over on their way up the ladder."

A look of righteous anger slowly worked its way across Frank's irregular features. "Come to think of it, it was down to Toby that we were at that bloody school in the first place if it wasn't for 'im insisting we walked through those fucking horrible woods, 'e wouldn't be dead now would 'e? Should've stuck with my plan, I told 'im, but would 'e listen to a goon like me?" he looked back at Hannah with a humorless grin, "Ha! Would 'e bollocks."

"And I'm sure your plan was far superior in its tactical strategy," Bronk agreed, "as you clearly are a man of action, not some lickspittle executive wannabe like your late, misguided friend."

Frank frowned uneasily at the word "lickspittle", not sure that he liked the sound of it being applied to Toby, even if he had gotten them into this. "I don't know about that, but it was a better plan and it wouldn't 'ave got Toby killed," he said in a sulky voice.

"What was your plan, Frank, I'm curious," asked Hannah, "if you don't mind giving away the tricks of the trade, that is..?"

"Oh well, you know, I would've gone for the straight ambush option meself," said Frank, assuming the tone of a craftsman explaining arcane secrets to an eager novice, "we could've just driven right past you and you never would've known, see? Then we could've stopped and waited for you. Somewhere nice and secluded like, then, when you turned up we could've hit you with the stinger we've got in the back…"

"Stinger?" Bronk asked, raising his eyebrows, "what's a stinger?"

"Big spiky thing you chuck in the road to burst tyres," said Frank, rolling his eyes and shaking his head in disgust, "don't you people know anything?"

"Sorry Frank, go on, this is all fascinating," apologized Bronk, "the insight into the mind of an expert like you is invaluable."

He looked at their new accomplice with an encouraging expression and Frank grudgingly continued. "I'd 'ave waited on a quiet bit of road, slung the stinger out and stopped that fancy tart's car of yours," he grinned nastily at Hannah, "then we could've just stood there and blasted away 'til we was sure you was dead. No risk, no problem, see?"

Frank seemed rather pleased with himself, then he noticed the looks of horror on Hannah and Bronk's faces and had the decency to look slightly sheepish. "Obviously, now I'm working for you," he said hurriedly, "that's not on the cards anymore, just, you know, illustratin' the sort of fing what we could've done."

"But, weren't you asked to bring us back in one piece?" Hannah asked, "Didn't Forrester tell you he needed us alive?"

"Nope," said Frank, "as long as we got that precious box, then you were..." he screwed up his forehead, "ex-pen-dibble and we were to make sure no-one found the bodies, that was all."

"So Forrester has found a way to re-open the rift then?" Bronk sounded worried, "How was he going to do that, did he get the generator running in Marvin's lab?"

"Don't know about that," said Frank, "they never tell me nothing about what they're up to. I only know 'e was planning to use that contraption to make trouble for that Calderwood bloke, something to do with 'is family, I reckon."

"I think we had better get back in touch with Marvin as soon as possible." said Bronk, slowing the car as they approached a junction, "which way to your hideout Frank?"

"Take a left and keep going for a mile or so," Frank replied, "there's a greasy spoon off the main road, you can buy me lunch like you promised," he glanced into the back seat, "and I expect the bitc... I mean Hannah, could do with some grub too?"

"Yes, This bitch could most definitely do with some grub, thank you Frank, you're very thoughtful." Hannah smiled sweetly and held Frank's gaze until he grunted and turned back to Bronk.

"When we've eaten, the lockup is about ten minutes down the road, you can ring your mate from there," he looked around once more at the strange looking telephone in the box on the back seat, "or whatever you do with that fing."

A few minutes later, Bronk took the turn Frank indicated and they drove down a short, narrow road that opened into a car park in front of single story building, with a large neon sign on the roof that read Big Ed's Place in flickering red letters, barely visible in the hazy sunshine.

There were two cars parked outside the diner, but no other signs of life that Bronk could see. He stopped, switched off the engine and sat in silence, listening and looking around. Then he got out, signaled for Frank to follow him but held up his hand when Hannah opened her door, meaning she should stay in the car until they'd made sure the place was safe.

"Sod that," she said, "I'm not staying out here on my own, you never know who might try to sneak up on me," she looked pointedly at Frank, "besides, I'm too hungry to wait any longer."

She got out and slammed the car door. "Lead me to the food."

The three of them walked into the almost empty restaurant like they were cowboys making a dramatic entrance into a Wild West saloon, pausing in the doorway and scoping the place out before heading for the counter.

A man in a rumpled suit, his tie and top button undone – traveling salesman, thought Bronk – was sitting alone at the far end of the room, reading a newspaper while eating a huge fried breakfast and taking occasional, noisy slurps of coffee.

He didn't even seem to register their presence and the only other customer, sitting in a booth by the door, was a spotty teenager in ripped jeans and oil-stained denim jacket and he appeared to be asleep, his head tipped over the top of his high- backed seat, eyes closed, mouth open.

"Hello folks, what can I do you for?"

A short woman of indefinable age, somewhere between 45 and 70, with a ruddy complexion and steel grey hair in a blue net, came through a door behind the counter, wearing the universal outfit of an apron and checked trousers worn by cooks everywhere. When she stopped dead and her friendly face burst into a beaming smile.

"Frankie! As I live and breath! You haven't been in for the longest time, I thought you'd moved on and forgotten us. Come here and give your aunty Edwina a hug, you big bear."

Frank gave Bronk and Hannah a look that conveyed quite clearly what the consequences would be for making a comment at this point, then leaned over the counter and enveloped Edwina, who Hannah assumed was "Big Ed", in a surprisingly tender embrace and kissed her on top of her tightly-netted head.

"Hello Ed," Frank released her and smiled shyly, something Hannah didn't think he was capable of, "I've been working away, sorry. I meant to get out here but Toby and me, we've been busy."

He looked at Bronk apologetically, "Could we have three of your mixed grills please love and we're in a bit of a rush, if that's ok."

Big Ed looked at Frank's companions and said, "Aren't you going to introduce me to your friends, Frankie, or have you forgotten your manners?"

"Sorry, um," Frank looked embarrassed, "Ed, this is my, er, my friend, Hannah, and Bronk, um, Mr. Bronk I mean…"

"Just Bronk is perfectly adequate, thank you, Frankie." Bronk grinned at the big man's suddenly frozen smile, "Delighted to make your acquaintance madam, any friend of Frankie's is a friend of ours, of course. May I also introduce you to my colleague, Ms. Hannah Meredith," he bowed his head in her direction and Hannah nodded politely to Ed, "and I must say, a mixed grill sounds just the ticket for three hungry travellers, thank you."

"Pleased to meet you, I'm sure," said Ed, eyeing them cautiously, "go and sit down and I'll get cooking right away. You want coffee? Tea?"

"Coffee please, Ed, lots of coffee," said Hannah, "and thank you."

The three of them moved to a booth in the corner and sat waiting in thoughtful silence, well, Bronk and Hannah did, Frank just sat in ordinary silence, until Bronk turned to Frank and spoke very quietly. "That young man over there," he nodded to the sleeping, denim-clad kid by the door, "does he look like he's breathing to you?"

Frank studied the skinny figure in the booth across the room for a moment and frowned, then stood up and made his way over there, all the while keeping his eyes on the kid's chest. He couldn't see the rise and fall of his ribs under the grubby jacket, even when he stopped in front of the booth, so Frank leaned over and nudged the kid on the shoulder. "Hey kid, wake up."

"Not going to happen, Frank."

Frank turned at the sound of the unfamiliar voice, hearing Hannah's gasp from behind him, as they both belatedly noticed the scruffy businessman at the far end of the room watching them, the silenced pistol in his hand resting on the tabletop, unwaveringly leveled at Frank's head.

"Who the fuck are you?" asked Frank, a perfectly reasonable question, Hannah thought.

"Did you top this kid? What are you, some kinda fucking psycho?"

"No Frank, I'm the replacement for you and that useless fuckwit, Toby," the man sneered, "consider yourself retired."

Then he raised the gun and fired two shots in quick succession at Frank.

The first one caught him in the side; Hannah saw a puff of red as the bullet clipped him and saw splinters fly from a table behind him as the bullet continued its trajectory. The second shot went wide, smashing the window to the right of Bronk and Hannah's table, but by then Frank was moving.

Hannah had read a lot of pulpy thrillers in her time and she was all too familiar with the "for a big man, he moved surprisingly quickly" cliché, but this was the first time she'd experienced it in the flesh, so to speak.

Frank charged at the gunman, that was the only way to describe it. He roared too, a scary sound, even when she wasn't on the receiving end of it, an incoherent explosion of fury so loud and unexpected that the hitman stumbled backward over his chair and the third shot went in the ceiling.

Then Frank was on him. Fists windmilling furiously, despite his broken fingers, he connected with the man's shocked face several times in the space of a few seconds, knocking him back over the table with blood spraying from his smashed nose, landing in a heap against the far wall. But he was on his feet again only seconds later and he still had the gun.

He grinned through the blood covering his face and raised the pistol, the long bulbous silencer pointed at Frank's heart. "Bye Frank, I can't say it's been a pleasure."

"You can say that again," said Big Ed.

The man spun around, the gun in his hand swinging toward the counter at the sound of her voice, but he wasn't fast enough.

A sawn-off shotgun is a deadly efficient weapon at close range and the one Ed fired at him from a distance of about ten feet was no exception; his head was practically vaporized by the blast and the second barrel caught him in the chest, hurling him back against the wall and making a hole the size of a dinner plate in his ribcage.

There was silence for a few seconds, broken only by the sound of muffled gagging from Hannah's direction.

"Thanks Ed," said Frank, almost calmly, "I thought I was a gonner for a minute there."

"Little fucker thinks he can come in here, killing my customers, what does he expect?" she said, "Who was he anyway, the competition?"

"No, I reckon I may 'ave picked the wrong side this time," said Frank "the sort what doesn't take kindly to you leaving the business, if you know what I mean?"

Big Ed looked over at Hannah and Bronk, still frozen in their seats, staring at the bloody mess in the corner with wide eyes and horrified expressions.

"I reckon you three should be on your way, how's that scratch, Frankie?"

Frank twisted to look at the hole in his side and grimaced, clutching his stiffening chest muscles. "Pah, bloody cricket ball injury hurts more," Big Ed gave him a puzzled look, "Long story, I'll tell you another time," he said, "we need to get the fuck out of here, sharpish."

"Wait, I'll not have you going hungry," Ed vanished into the kitchen for two minutes, then came back carrying a loaf of bread and a large foil parcel, "It's only cold sausages and a few chicken legs, but it'll give you something to snack on. Can't have my Frankie wasting away can we?" She reached up and affectionately pinched Frank's cheek, and much to Hannah's amusement, Frank blushed.

"Thank you Ed," Bronk said, "I'm sorry to have caused you such an inconvenience."

"Just you look after my Frankie," she replied, staring at

him with eyes as hard as flint, "that's all the thanks I need from you."

"It's a deal." Bronk took the still-shaken Hannah gently by the arm and guided her past the bloody carnage to the door of the restaurant, where Frank was impatiently peering out into the car park.

"All looks clear at the moment, time to go," he said, his face set in a stony mask.

"We need to be somewhere safe where we can get organized," he raised a hand to Big Ed in farewell then turned back to Bronk and Hannah, "and then we're going to find Forrester and make him fucking pay for this."

16
Turning the Tables

The short drive from Big Ed's Place to Frank's hideout was made in tense silence. Frank stared grimly through the windscreen and Bronk gripped the wheel with a fierce intensity, constantly glancing in the rear view mirror to check they weren't being followed.

They all agreed since the hitman had been waiting for them at the diner, it was unlikely Forrester and his band of villains knew the exact location of their former employee's hideout. They were gambling that they'd be safe there, providing they could get there undetected.

"Turn right up here," breaking the silence, Frank pointed out the entrance to a small business park, "slow down when you reach the second unit, but don't stop, I want to check it out first."

Bronk did as Frank asked, slowly cruising past the steel-clad industrial units and following the road round, passing a few still trading on Saturday afternoon but most were closed for the weekend. Frank scanned the front of his own lockup as they passed and could see no sign of forced entry, the padlock on the roller door seemed to be in place and the windows were all intact.

The road brought them back around in a circle and as they once more approached the park's entrance, Frank told Bronk to pull over. Getting out, he walked quickly to the front of the anonymous building and stooped to unlock the padlock from its ring in the floor. He rolled the door up and peered into the shadowy interior, seemed satisfied nothing was amiss and gestured for Bronk to drive the Range Rover inside.

As soon as the car came to a stop, Frank rolled the shutter down behind it and switched on the lights, illuminating a surprisingly tidy, well organised workshop. The main floor space was surrounded by workbenches and a large selection of tools, all spotless and laid out on stenciled shadow boards. There was a door to a corner office, glazed on two sides, with a metal stairway leading above it to a mezzanine level, which held storage racks and a kitchen area equipped with a sink, a kettle, and small electric stove.

Hannah and Bronk climbed out of the car and looked around.

"Nice place you've got here," said Hannah, "I'm impressed Frank, you're full of surprises."

"I've 'ad it a few years now," Frank replied, "I used to be in the motor trade, see? Used to do tune-ups, conversion jobs and all sorts in 'ere, 'til I met Toby and 'e got me involved with those fucking psychos," a look of sadness crossed his face, "and look where that fucking got us. Toby dead and me on the run."

"Well maybe that's something you can go back to after we're done with all this," said Hannah, not unkindly, "it's always good to have a skill you can fall back on." Frank just grunted non-committally and led the way to his office.

Inside, there was a modern desk, three comfortable swivel chairs and what looked to be a state of the art computer setup. On a purpose built workstation, it ran along one complete wall of the room under the windows looking out onto the floor of the main building.

"Just had all this lot put in a couple of months back," Frank indicated the chairs and went to turn on the computer, entering a password and powering up the dual monitors before turning back to them, "I'll heat up the grub Ed gave us, make yourselves comfy," he made for the stairs, "who's for coffee?"

"That would be most appreciated, thank you, Frank,"

Hannah smiled at him, starting to feel like she could relax for the first time in what seemed like a long time, "do you need any help?"

"I'll be fine, thanks anyway love," Frank managed a twisted grin, "I'm quite domesticated, believe it or not."

He turned to Bronk, "Whatever you need to do with that," he nodded at the box containing the timephone, "be my guest, I won't be long."

When Frank had gone, Hannah collapsed into a chair with a heavy sigh and kicked off her boots. "So, what do you think, are we safe here?"

Bronk considered her question while unpacking the box, fitting the adaptor onto the cable and searching for a socket to connect Marvin's chronophonic device to the phone network.

"I'm not sure about safe exactly, but we should certainly use this brief respite wisely. Ah, here we are," he plugged the cable into the wall socket and did some fine tuning to the phone's controls, "that should do it."

The now familiar, hollow metallic echo reverberated from the high end speakers attached to the powerful computer system for a few seconds and Bronk adjusted the volume slightly, lowering it still further when Marvin Calderwood's voice boomed across the room.

"Hello, is that you Bronk? Miss Meredith, Hannah, are you there?"

"We're here Marvin," answered Bronk. Frank reappeared from upstairs, carrying a tray of sandwiches and coffee, "and we have a new companion with us too, say hello, Frank."

"Hello," Frank replied, eyeing the peculiar looking phone suspiciously, "who are you then, another friend of Forrester's who got on the wrong side of 'im are you?"

"To whom am I speaking?" asked Marvin. *"Are you another old friend of Hannah's?"*

"Nmoff efbrakly." Hannah swallowed the mouthful of

sausage sandwich she'd been chewing and tried again. "Excuse me. Not exactly, Marvin, more like a new recruit to the cause. Frank is a former employee of Forrester's, who has now seen the error of his ways." She looked at the scowling ex-goon and grinned. "Isn't that right, Frank?"

"I've 'ad a change of 'eart, it's true," said Frank, "yer man Bronk 'ere, 'e made me a better offer. Anyway, those toffs are a bunch of cu…"

"Thank you, Frank," cut in Bronk smoothly, "I'm sure Marvin gets the idea. Would you be good enough to pour me a coffee?"

Frank's scowl deepened, "I'm not a fucking waiter, pour it yourself." He picked up his own mug, grabbed a chicken leg off the tray and headed for the door. "I'm going to check what gear Toby packed in the back of the Rover," he turned as he reached the door, "if that's ok with you, Mr. Bronk..?" When Bronk only shook his head, Frank left, slamming the door behind him.

"Touchy." said Hannah, laughing, "I think you upset our new friend, Bronk."

"Who was that, that…person?" asked Marvin primly. *"What type of barbarians have you thrown in with, Bronk, why have you sought out this thug's assistance?"*

"That's not important, Marvin," said Hannah, "what we need to know now is can we prevent Forrester from gaining control of those last few companies he needs to complete his financial power base in time?"

"Marvin, we believe he may have already discovered how to operate one of your generators," Bronk cut in, "he may well be planning to send back a team to retrieve the relevant information and obtain the necessary patents, which would render you obsolete, as far as Forrester is concerned."

"The scoundrel!" The anger in Marvin's voice was clear. *"I'll not sit here, placidly awaiting my execution, what is it you need me to do?"*

"I have calculated the next window of opportunity for us to enter the rift," said Bronk, consulting a notebook he took from his coat pocket, "we would need to be forty miles east of our current location by 4.35 on Sunday morning, so we'd really need to be on the ball, that's only," Bronk looked at his watch, "thirteen hours from now. We would need to have somewhere to connect the device so we could send the anchoring signal, unless..." Bronk began searching through the neatly bunched cables behind the computer equipment until he found what he was looking for, then traced a single cable to its source and disconnected it. "I think I may have found a solution to that problem. Hannah, may I borrow your mobile phone please?"

She passed him her battered smartphone and watched as he connected one end of the cable to the micro USB port, then took the other end and stood by the timephone.

"Marvin, we are going to lose the connection for a moment, I shall contact you again shortly."

Before Marvin had a chance to reply, Bronk unplugged the timephone's cable and detached the adaptor. He studied the various configurations on top and then plugged the cable from Hannah's phone into the matching socket.

Almost instantly, a tinny echo was audible from the small speaker in Hannah's phone, *"Hello? Are you there?"*

Hannah was impressed. "We are indeed Marvin. Bronk had a flash of inspiration and I believe we now have ourselves a portable wormhole attractor...or whatever it is," she looked at Bronk and shrugged, "it's as good a name as any." They agreed to contact Marvin again when they arrived at the predicted location of the rift the following morning.

When Frank returned from doing his inventory of the car, his mood was much improved. He had discovered a variety of automatic weapons and handy explosive devices the ever-vigilant Toby had thoughtfully, if unknowingly, provided for them. Once they had a full inventory of what they had to work with, they spent the next couple of hours honing the details of their plan before turning in for the night.

Frank insisted on keeping watch, while Bronk dozed in a chair, saying he would take over later. Hannah made herself comfortable in the reclining front seat of the Rover and was asleep almost at once.

She was awoken by Bronk gently shaking her shoulder and holding a steaming mug of coffee under her nose. It was a testament to her newly relaxed mental state that she didn't have a heart attack, or at the very least, punch him in the face, so the few precious hours sleep and the food must have helped.

Frank even had a spare toothbrush, handing it to her with comically sincere assurances of its unused state. She managed to freshen up enough at the small sink to feel nearly human again by the time they climbed into the car at 3:30 a.m. on Sunday and pulled out of Frank's hideout, heading into a dark and uncertain future.

17
Contact

The small village was dark and silent as Bronk drove down the narrow high street. The protruding thatched eaves of the stone cottages on either side made it feel claustrophobic, deserted and somehow sinister. When the Range Rover emerged into the open countryside again, Bronk was glad to see the crescent moon reappear overhead.

Hannah leaned forward between the front seats, holding the map she'd been following. Frank had printed it from the internet before they left, along with a few other things that would be essential to their plan, and pointed out the turning up ahead. "We need to follow that track for about two miles, it should lead us down to a small river in the woods, the rift is due to pass through there in half an hour."

"Great, more bloody woods," grumbled Frank, "what is this, a sodding nature trail, or what?"

Hannah ignored him, instead, she checked to make sure her phone was fully charged before disconnecting it from the car charger. When she was finished, she turned to Bronk, "When we get down there, how long will we be able to keep the rift open for, do you think?"

"Theoretically," said Bronk, "it should remain stable for as long as the phone's battery holds out, it only needs the anchor signal to keep it locked to this location. But this isn't an exact science, not by any stretch of the imagination, so we will need to exercise extreme caution and make sure we return as soon as possible, in case the rift collapses and we become stranded."

"One of us should stay 'ere," said Frank, "otherwise some sneaky fucker could get 'ere and hang up on us, then we'd be properly screwed wouldn't we?"

Bronk thought about this for a moment before replying, "You are right of course, Frank, and as our head of security I think it should be you who is responsible for that. 'Establish a perimeter' or whatever it is you security chaps say and ensure nobody creeps up on us. Not until we're ready for them, anyway."

Frank's face positively glowed with pride. "Head of security, I like that," he said with a crooked grin, "never been head of anyfing before."

"Well, I have every faith in your ability to keep us safe," said Hannah, "anyone would think twice before tackling a dedicated professional like you. You're the ultimate deterrent."

Bronk slowed when they reached a gate marking the end of the track. Stopping the car, he climbing out into the chilly pre-dawn gloom and searched for the latch. Finding it, he swung open the old wooden gate and returned to the comfort of the Rover's heated interior. He drove slowly forward until he cleared the gate, then got out and closed it behind them, listening briefly for any sounds of pursuit before hurrying back to the car.

It was only another few minutes drive until the gently sloping field levelled out and merged gradually with an area of mature woodland that followed the snaking path of the river. There was plenty of space between the trunks of the ancient trees for Bronk to navigate around and very little of the type of tangled undergrowth Frank had fought his way through, only twenty-four hours ago with his late co-worker, Toby.

Bronk turned on the dashboard mounted satellite navigation system for this final part of the journey, wanting to position them as precisely in line with the path of the rift as possible.

When the coordinates on the glowing screen matched the scrawled figures in his notebook, Bronk stopped the car and turned off the engine. They all sat for a moment without speaking, peering out at the occasional shards of moonlight that broke through the tree canopy, making strange, angular shapes in the shadows on the leafy woodland floor, until Frank eventually took the initiative and got out, closing the door behind him.

He walked around to the back of the car and opened the tailgate, lifted the spare wheel out of its storage well and laid it on the ground, then felt around until he located a hidden catch, which he twisted, revealing a compartment underneath. Unclipping a torch from its bracket, Frank shone it into the dark space. Reaching in, he brought out a large, dangerous-looking handgun and a silencer, which he dropped into the pocket of his jacket. He checked the pistol was fully loaded and took two extra magazines from Toby's secret arms stash, then closed the tailgate and returned to the front of the car.

Frank opened the passenger door and spoke with an authority Hannah hadn't heard before. "Stay here, both of you," he looked at his watch, "we've still got fifteen minutes, I just wanna check that nobody followed us, capiche?"

"Of course, Frank," said Bronk, "but don't go too far, we may need to leave at quite short notice."

When he had closed the door and disappeared into the woods, Hannah looked at Bronk grimaced. "Capiche", really? I think Frank's promotion may have gone to his head, hahaha."

Bronk gave her an amused shrug and began unpacking the box, assembling the timephone and attaching Hannah's mobile to it with the USB cable. When he had everything set up, he took the other sheets Frank had printed for them out of the rapidly disintegrating cardboard box, slipped them into his pocket and turned to Hannah. "Ok, this is it, are you ready?"

"Ready as I'll ever be," she said, "which is to say, no, not really, but I'm going to do it anyway."

"That's good enough for me," Bronk reassured her, "and, to be honest, a lot more than I have any right to expect of you, so thank you."

"Hey, Sundays are always so boring anyway," Hannah replied with a smile and more than a little bravado, "what else would I be doing?"

Bronk carefully placed the two connected phones back in the bottom of the box and opened the car door, just as Frank reappeared out of the slowly lightening dawn, carrying something over his shoulder and looking very smug. He walked up and unceremoniously dumped the heavy shape in a heap on the ground. It was a body.

"What did I tell yer," he said with some satisfaction, "I found this," he kicked the unmoving figure, "skulking around in the woods back there," he jerked a thumb over his shoulder, " 'e never knew what hit 'im."

"Is he…?" began Hannah.

"Dead? Yeah, 'e's dead alright, smacked 'im with a bloody great rock d'in't I? I always say. you can't make an omelette without cracking heads. Well 'e shouldn'a been making fucking omelettes on my watch, should 'e?"

"Eggs", Frank, it's "without breaking eggs"", said Hannah weakly, only now noticing the rather unconventional shape of their erstwhile observer's skull, "but I take your point, he was asking for trouble, trying to sneak up on you." Then, as an afterthought, she added, "Just remind me to never ask you to make me an omelette, that's all."

Frank grinned and reached into his pocket, bringing out a small radio and a revolver. "Sneaky little bastard was carrying these. And 'e's got binoculars too."

He leaned down and untangled a leather strap from around the man's neck, lifting free an odd-shaped pair of field glasses and handing all three items to Bronk.

Bronk made a quick inspection of the gun and radio, both of which vanished into the capacious pockets of his coat before turning his attention to the glasses. "Well, it seems our unfortunate friend here was very well prepared." he adjusted the controls and handed them to Hannah, who took them and looked through the eyepieces, gasping in surprise at what she saw.

"He was using night vision glasses to keep watch on us, which suggests to me that Forrester and his goons won't be far behind since he was obviously keeping them updated by radio."

Hannah looked at her watch through the light-intensifying glasses and realised it was almost time.

"We need to get ready," she said, "the rift will be arriving any minute. We have to call Marvin and let him know."

Bronk powered up Hannah's mobile, then turned on Marvin Calderwood's extraordinary invention and waited until the sound of metallic hissing issued from the speaker before taking a deep breath and trying to reestablish contact. "Hello Marvin, can you hear me?"

"Loud and clear." The excitement was apparent in Marvin's voice straight away. *"Are you all prepared at that end? I have the generator running already, just say the word and I will increase the output to full power on your command."*

"Hold on Marvin," said Bronk. He took the box from where he'd left it on the Range Rover's bonnet and walked several paces from the car before placing it on the ground. "Ok," he said after taking a step back, "power it up whenever you're ready."

"Increasing output now... passing 60%." Hannah thought she could just hear a rising hum in the background, as Marvin continued to count. *"70%...80%... 90%...the generator is now at full power and I'm going to*

open the rift...Now!"

For a second, Hannah thought nothing would happen, then a shrill whistling noise made them cover their ears, followed by what looked like a slow motion bolt of lightning that zig-zagged up from the box until it was about six feet long. It just hung there in the air, like a snake responding to the music of a fakir's flute, mesmerising by its very presence.

The jagged, eerily silent strip of light hovered impossibly over the box for nearly a minute before the spell was broken by Marvin's voice, *"Hello? Hannah? Bronk, are you still there?"*

"Sorry Marvin, we're here," Bronk replied, finally managing to tear his eyes away from the eldritch glow, "the rift has materialised, but it does not seem to have fully opened, I may need to make some fine adjustments to your device."

"For God's sake man, be careful," Marvin said. *"On no account must you come in contact with the rift before it..."* His voice disappeared in a loud burst of static, returning only long enough for them to catch a few distorted words. *"... could be fatal... stuck in between..."* Then the audio signal cut out altogether.

Bronk looked at Hannah and Frank. "It seems we have no choice," he said, "please remain here while I attempt to make the necessary alterations to the signal frequency."

"But Marvin was trying to warn you," said Hannah, "he was definitely worried and I didn't like the sound of what he was saying about you getting stuck somewhere."

"No, and even I know what "fatal" means." rumbled Frank glaring with malicious distrust at the frozen lightning bolt that was still standing, against all probability, rigidly upright in the battered cardboard box. "And that sounds a fuck sight worse than being stuck anywhere to me."

Hannah and Bronk exchanged another look, Bronk

shrugged and smiled, reached out and absently patted her arm, then turned and walked towards the box and the glowing rift.

Stepping within a few feet of the box, he felt the hairs on his scalp and arms trying to stand on end, caught the unmistakable smell of ozone and heard a harsh fizzing, crackling noise coming from the rift. The box was brightly lit from within, the single word, Stuff, standing out clearly against the translucent cardboard for a final few seconds before it disintegrated completely, leaving the eye-watering gash in spacetime hanging over the conjoined telephones like some sort of trans-dimensional damoclean icicle.

Bronk heard Hannah gasp behind him as the box collapsed in on itself, but he forced himself to ignore everything else and focused all his concentration on the timephone. He crouched down, shading his eyes from the blinding glare with one hand, and reaching with the other into the narrow gap between buzzing streak of light and the ground, inching toward the dial on the phone.

Which was when the rift moved.

Hannah held her breath as she watched Bronk stretch out his arm to adjust the phone, his figure only visible as a stark silhouette against the painful whiteness of the light. Then, suddenly, the entire rift seemed to jab downwards, as though attracted to the presence of Bronk's hand beneath it and, before either she or Frank had time to think, let alone react, Bronk was gone.

18
Past Imperfect

At first, Hannah just stared in amazement at the space Bronk had so recently occupied, because her mind was simply unable to comprehend his sudden disappearance. Then her legs seemed to take on a life of their own and she half-ran, half-stumbled towards the hissing, crackling white light of the rift, still hanging completely immobile above the two interconnected phones where they lay on the ground, in the centre of the small leafy clearing. She wasn't sure what she intended to do when she got there, but fortunately for her, their newly promoted head of security chose this moment to intervene.

"Hey!" said Frank, grabbing Hannah's wrist as she zombie-walked past him. "Where the bloody 'ell d'you fink you're going?" She spun around and stared at him, her eyes wide and unfocused, still pulling against the iron grip he had on her arm, trying desperately to get to the rift.

Like a sleepwalker, thought Frank, she doesn't know what she's doing. He screwed up his considerable forehead, the only external sign of a complex moral dilemma that raged inside what we shall have to refer to as Frank's conscience, at least, until someone comes up with a more appropriate term. His Mum had always told him it was bad to hit girls, especially ones who, against all the odds, hadn't turned out to be complete bitches but, well, there was a time and a place for morals…

"Sorry, Miss," said Frank, with apparent deference, "but it's for your own good." And then he slapped her, quite hard.

"Ow! Fuck! What did you do that for?" Hannah looked

down to where Frank's giant swollen paw engulfed her wrist, the livid, cricket ball-shaped bruise now a psychedelic mix of purple, crimson and black, with a hint of yellow around the edges.

"And why are you crushing my arm..?" Hannah stopped and slowly turned to look at the hovering white slash of eye-twisting light. Then she turned back to Frank. "Bronk, what happened to Bronk? We have to go after him!"

"You don't really fink I'm going to let you do something that fucking stupid, do you?" said Frank. "Mr. Bronk would have my bollocks off if I let you go through there on your own, and besides," he gave her a sly grin, "you're the one who said one of us 'as to stay 'ere and I'm not leaving you 'ere on your own either, so you're stuck with me until we hear otherwise from Mr. Bronk."

Hannah opened her mouth to protest further, but seeing Frank's expression she knew it was pointless to argue so she gave up, for now anyway. "Fine," she said, yanking her arm forcibly from Frank's grip and rubbing her wrist.

"We shall just have to hope Bronk reached Marvin's lab and they have enough time to set things up before Forrester finds out where we are." She looked up at Frank. "In the meantime, you and I have got things to do."

Hannah glanced back once more at the eerily glowing tear in the fabric of the world and whispered, "Good luck, my friend, I think we're all going to need it." Then she and Frank returned to the car to prepare for the final stage of their plan.

If had been a surprise for Hannah and Frank, then you would need a whole new word to describe the sensation Bronk felt, as he blinked out of existence in the pre-dawn light of a home counties woodland and was flung down the snaking tube of the wormhole.

The structure of the wormhole, if you could call it that,

seemed to be both real and unreal at the same time. It appeared solid enough from within, enough that it was impossible to see anything beyond the speeding, iridescent white wall of the wildly spiralling space-time corridor, but when Bronk's tumbling figure came in contact with whatever made up the body of the tube, he felt no resistance whatsoever; his hands and feet sometimes vanished into the surface of the wall to a depth of several inches without sustaining any obvious injury.

After a few failed attempts to slow his erratic, disorienting progress, it occurred to Bronk that maybe it wasn't him that was moving, but rather it was the wormhole itself, twisting and deforming around him. He closed his eyes and almost immediately, without the crazily spinning visual input as his point of reference, the nauseous feeling of motion sickness retreated and he could gather his thoughts.

Bronk had no recall of the first journey he had made through the rift, just the fuzzy memories of throbbing pain in his head and of waking up in a strange new world that seemed all the more different for its familiarity with what he thought of as "home". So this time, he concentrated as hard as he could on noting any physical or sensory details that may prove useful, which was what he was doing when his journey ended, as abruptly as it had begun.

He had no way of telling how long the trip through the wormhole took, time here seemed elastic and inconsequential and it made his mind ache, just trying to think how long he had been floating in its silent embrace. Then time suddenly came back with an almost audible SNAP and Bronk found himself kneeling on a cold stone floor, breathing in the somehow comforting smell of burning ozone and hearing a gasp, followed by the reassuring sound of a very familiar voice.

"Oh, thank God for that." said Marvin Calderwood, "My dear Bronk, I don't believe I have ever been so pleased to see anyone in my entire life."

Bronk squinted in the harsh light of the arc lamps which lit Marvin's laboratory and shakily got to his feet. He shaded his eyes against the glare and could just make out a figure at the far end of the room, behind a bank of control levers and thick coils of heavy electrical cable. He took a few unsteady paces and, as his eyes became accustomed to the brightness of the room, the features of his old friend and mentor swam into focus.

"Marvin, you took the words right out of my mouth," replied Bronk with a smile, "but I'm afraid we're going to have to postpone the reunion celebrations until later, we have only a short while before our guests arrive and we need time to prepare."

He reached the console where Marvin stood and gave the old engineer a warm hug, before pulling back to study him and take note of the dark bags beneath Marvin's eyes and the deeply drawn lines on a face that had aged in a way that shocked his faithful assistant.

For, although Bronk and Marvin had spent many years in their respective futures, they now met at virtually the same point in time and space where they had created the first generator, the very one which was humming loudly in its protective cabinet behind the control console, the dials and gauges showing it was still running at maximum power.

It was a strange feeling, standing in a room you knew so well, in a time you remember from long ago as if the future and the past were all rolled into one. Bronk found it hard to reconcile the fact that he and Marvin were so much older and yet here they stood, in the place they had first made their momentous discovery as relatively young men. It was best not to think about it unless you wanted to end up going out of your mind.

Bronk pulled the folded sheets of paper out of his pocket and placed them on Marvin's chipped and stained desk. "How do you think these look, Marvin," he asked, "do you think they'll fool people for long enough?"

Marvin picked up one of the printed sheets and studied it closely for a minute or two. Then he screwed it up and dropped it on the floor, where he proceeded to grind it into the grubby stones with the heel of his boot. He picked it up and unfolded the creased and dirty page, which he once more smoothed on the tabletop. "Now they will be fine," he smiled, "they don't want to appear too new, after all."

"Good thinking," agreed Bronk, "we should get to it, where do you suggest we put them..?"

"Can you see anything?" The voice was impatient, on edge. "Have you had any contact with Roberts, he said he'd tracked them to the woods didn't he?"

"There's definitely something, I can see some sort of weird glow coming from down there, but I've had no word from Roberts, and the team I sent on ahead haven't seen him." The man lowered his night vision glasses and turned to Forrester, standing with his hands thrust into the pockets of his expensive raincoat. "It's like he just vanished into thin air."

Forrester's expression was tense and angry, his face still clearly suffering from his encounter with Hannah at the cottage. Two black eyes and a badly swollen nose, along with a lump the size of a golf ball on his forehead were evidence of his collision with the fireplace, but the blazing fury in his eyes was all reserved for Hannah herself.

Paul Forrester had developed an obsessive and all-consuming hatred for that bloody Meredith woman, all she'd done since the very first time they'd met was to get in his fucking way and complicate his life. He should have killed her at the auction and saved himself all this grief.

Well, now he had the bitch cornered and this time there

was no way she was going to slip through his fingers, her and that weasel, Bronk, neither of them were going to leave those woods alive, he promised himself that if nothing else.

"Right, we're going down there," he said, climbing into his SUV, "I'm not waiting any longer. Tell everyone I want Hannah Meredith alive, anybody else you find down there, kill them."

19
Best Laid Plans

Paul Forrester had carefully mapped out his approach to the clearing in the woods. As an added precaution he also sent men down the opposite side of the valley to cross the small river and provide flanking cover, in case their quarry tried to make a break for it when he and his personal protection squad arrived to take care of the irritant that was Hannah bloody Meredith, once and for all.

He kept in radio contact with the teams already in the area where she and Bronk had last been sighted, where the bright glow had been seen by everyone. Although the only illumination now was from the slowly creeping dawn and the occasional snatch of light from the moon from behind the massing clouds of an impending storm front. Thunder could already be heard in the distance and a few heavy drops of rain began to splatter the windscreen of Forrester's car.

"This is team two," his radio crackled on the dashboard, "no sign of them in this sector."

"Team four, nothing here so far either."

One by one, the other scouts reported in but nobody had seen anything and the strange glow they witnessed earlier had yet to put in another appearance.

Forrester angrily grabbed the radio and keyed the transmit button, "They cannot have just disappeared, FIND THEM!" He threw the handset back on the dash in disgust and turned to his silent, black-clad driver. "Get me down there, into the clearing, now. I'm obviously going to have to do this myself."

The man nodded, spoke quietly into a concealed

microphone and engaged the four-wheel drive, turning off the rough track and taking a direct route across the fields, heading for the coordinates pinpointed by the reconnaissance teams.

The rain was coming down harder now, the impact of it kicking up tiny explosions of soil and leaves from the ground. Even with the broken cover of branches overhead, Forrester's men were about as thrilled with outdoor pursuits as Frank and Toby had been the previous night. Wet and miserable, they weren't concentrating on much more than spotting the posh bitch and that weasely turncoat sidekick of hers. Which probably explained why the pile of leaves, banked up at the edge of the clearing like drifted snow, went unnoticed by all four sets of henchmen who searched there.

After the disgruntled muttering of the final group of goons had merged with the sounds of the storm, the pile moved and shifted, eventually resolving itself into the figure of Frank, leaves stuck to his face and hair, his clothes soaked through, rising out of the woodland floor like some sort of avenging demon, followed by the somewhat less intimidating shape of Hannah, bedraggled and exhausted.

"You ok?" Frank asked, hauling Hannah to her feet. "I reckon they've gone, told you they wouldn't look too hard din't I? Now we've just got to hope that your mate Marvin sticks to the schedule."

"Yes," Hannah agreed, "and that Bronk made it back to the lab ok, he could have ended up anywhere."

Frank suddenly held up a hand, turning his head to listen through the pounding of the rain. "There's someone coming, I hear a motor," peering at his watch through the downpour, "and we have another ten minutes until we'll be ready for the bastard."

"Well then, we'll just have to keep him occupied won't we," replied Hannah, "this is our only chance to stop Forrester and I'll be damned if we've gone through all this, just to have him get his way now."

She looked toward the centre of the clearing, where the interconnected phones were no longer visible after Frank had placed them in a small depression in the ground, covering them with a tarp and a layer of leaves, where they remained undiscovered by the searchers.

"Bronk will come through for us, it'll be fine," she said. But she wondered who it was she was trying to convince.

At that moment, or at least the moment which coincided with that same moment, nearly two hundred years earlier, where it was also raining, Bronk and Marvin Calderwood were returning to the warm and dry comfort of Marvin's lab, having spent the last hour putting up the flyers made on Frank's computer. They had pasted them on doors, shop windows and lampposts; anywhere suitably conspicuous to ensure as many people would see them as possible, as a new day began and the city went about its business.

The posters were simple, with a basic, old-fashioned typeface and an intentionally grainy photo of Forrester, with the eye-catching caption:

WANTED FOR MURDER AND KIDNAPPING.

HAVE YOU SEEN THIS MAN? SUBSTANTIAL REWARD FOR INFORMATION.

followed by the handwritten address of the local police station and a warning Forrester was a dangerous criminal who was almost certainly armed.

Bronk took off his dripping coat and checked the time, realising they had barely five minutes until they were due to power up the generator again.

Marvin had turned it off ten minutes after Bronk had arrived, just enough time to make sure Hannah hadn't attempted to follow him, but not long enough that their pursuers could surprise them if they caught up with Hannah and Frank before they were ready.

Now, Bronk was nervous, biting his nails and constantly checking his watch, knowing that his friends were depending on him to get this right and aware that they wouldn't get a second chance.

Forrester's SUV drove slowly up to the edge of the clearing and came to a halt. His driver spent a minute scanning the murky surroundings through the streams of water running down the windows, despite the wipers whipping across the screen, then opened his door and climbed out into the storm.

"Wait here, sir," he said, "I'll check it out first." He closed the door and walked away from the car, vanishing into the sheets of rain as soon as he moved out of the narrow illuminated cone of the headlights, leaving Forrester to stare intently into the gloom.

Drawing his gun as he moved further into the open space amongst the trees, Forrester's bodyguard constantly looked around him, determined not to let his prey creep up on him, so he was startled when a figure staggered towards him out of the woods on the far side of the clearing.

It was the Meredith woman, he saw; she was soaked, covered in mud and clearly in a bad way, weaving and stumbling until she collapsed to her knees ten feet from him, a look of resignation in her eyes and all the fight gone from her expression.

He gave her a grim smile and raised his pistol, pointing

it at a spot in the centre of her forehead, "Say goodbye, bitch."

"Goodbye, bitch," said Hannah, with unexpected venom, grinning evilly at something over her executioner's shoulder.

The man spun around, just in time to meet Frank's giant, swollen fist coming the other way.

There was a noise like somebody flattening a nose, breaking cheekbones and shattering a jaw. Hannah was all out of analogies at this point and watched as the man went down like gravity had a grudge against him.

Frank grabbed the fallen thug under the arms and dragged him into the undergrowth, then looked at his watch and signalled to Hannah that it was almost time. "He ain't gonna 'ang about too long when his man don't come back," he warned. "Be ready. And don't worry, I've got you covered." With that, he nodded in encouragement and faded back into the trees, leaving Hannah alone once more.

The rain was beginning to ease off now and dawn was showing through the patches of grey cloud barely visible in the gaps of the spreading canopy of branches, making it easier to see beyond the trees that circled the clearing. Which was why Hannah spotted Paul Forrester walking towards her, the headlights of his car throwing his tall figure into sharp relief as he approached and reflecting off the blade of the long, evil-looking hunting knife he carried in his left hand.

He stopped when he reached the rough circle of open ground and looked around. "What have you done with my driver?" he asked in a casual voice. "Not that I need his assistance any longer, you understand, I'm simply curious."

Hannah said nothing, just glanced at her watch, then looked dispassionately back at Forrester, who took a few steps into the clearing and reached into his coat with the other hand, withdrawing a pistol. "I'm not going to make a big drama out of this, Ms. Meredith," he said with a sneer, "but I will give you a choice. You will tell me where the temporal device is, because if you don't, I shall go to work on you with this." he raised the knife, turning it this way and that to catch the light. "However, if you tell me what I want to know straight away, I will ensure your death is quick and painless," he brandished the gun, "it's entirely up to you."

When Hannah didn't respond, he took another step in her direction. "Very well, it makes very little difference to me either way…"

"Ok, it's time," said Bronk, as the second hand of his watch swept past the twelve.

"Start her up, Marvin."

He watched as his old friend threw switches and turned dials to increase power to the generator, the acrid smell of ozone filled the laboratory and Bronk readied himself, as near to where the rift would appear as he dared, clutching Marvin's pepperpot revolver.

Then, as the hum of the generator reached its high pitched peak, the eerie white light of the rift flooded into the lab and the two men braced themselves for whatever might happen next.

Forrester advanced on Hannah, her eyes fixed on the blade of his knife, knowing that if Bronk had failed in his attempt to reach Marvin, this could all be for nothing.

Then it happened; suddenly, between the two figures, the mesmerising, glowing slash in reality blinked back into existence and this time, it opened.

Hidden beneath their covering, the two phones had responded to Marvin's control and the signal forced the rift to appear as it had before, but this time Hannah saw it in its full form; a translucent disc, hanging in the air like a pool of liquid silver, ripples gently undulating over its surface in concentric rings, the shimmering, mirror-like circle obscuring Forrester from her view.

Watching from amongst the trees, Frank saw the rift flash open and knew this was his one chance. Rising from his hiding place as quietly as he could, Frank aimed for a point midway up the fucker's back and started to run.

The silver ring of the rift held Forrester's gaze as if he was in a trance, he'd waited so long for this moment. Now he could finally bring his plan to fruition and there was nobody left in his way to stop him.

Too late, he heard the sound of heavy footsteps behind him and turned, already bringing the gun up and firing wildly as Frank hurled himself in a desperate tackle, grabbing Forrester around the waist and ramming into him with his full weight, taking him over the threshold of the shining silver disc and disappearing into the void.

20
The Other Side

Marvin Calderwood watched intently as the gauges on the generator climbed into the red. When the system reached maximum power, he looked up to see that Bronk had taken up his position in the glare of the arc lamps at the end of the laboratory, then grasped a lever on the console and fixed his gaze on the sweeping second hand of his watch.

"Ready?" he asked, "Ten seconds…five, four, three…" Marvin took a deep breath. "Connecting now." And threw the switch.

The whine of the generator built to an almost unbearable level, then, just when Bronk thought he couldn't stand it any longer, the rift crackled into existence, tearing a zig-zag gash of hissing, spitting white light in the fabric of reality that was painfully bright, even under the lamps. After a short pause, the blinding rip in space-time blinked open, forming a shimmering silver disc which hung six inches above the stone floor, its surface undulating gently, like ripples on a pond.

"Maybe something went wro…" That was as far as Bronk got before the silver portal was forced violently outwards. Bulging like a sheet of rubber until the deformed surface snapped back into place and two wrestling figures were flung across the flagstones, accompanied by a handful of swirling leaves and a brief gust of wind.

Bronk trained the small, multi-barreled revolver on the two men, adjusting his aim as they struggled, trying to disentangle themselves from each other and the pile of cables on which they had come to rest.

"That's enough!" he shouted, "Please refrain from any more violence, or I shall be forced to shoot you."

"Ggrrrmmmpphh!" said one of the writhing combatants, adding, "Mnnffmmp Arrgh Fuuuck!" for emphasis, before grabbing his opponent's head and, impervious to Bronk's warning, he cracked it smartly on the floor, at which point the second man immediately went limp.

Only then did the victor stand up and raise his hands. "Alright, alright, no need to get your bollocks in a knot, don't shoot." Frank turned around with a grin. "Hello Mr. Bronk, fancy meetin' you 'ere."

Bronk lowered the pistol and sighed with relief. "Frank! What happened to Hannah, is she ok?"

"She'll be fine," Frank replied, looking curiously around the laboratory. "As long as she keeps 'er 'ead down and avoids the blokes this smarmy fucker sent after us," he jerked a thumb at the motionless heap at his feet, "but I reckon they'll give up pretty soon after they realise their boss is gone."

"Um…Hello?" Marvin had come out from behind the control console and stood with his hand out, looking nervously up at Frank. "Marvin Calderwood. I take it I have you to thank for helping keep Miss Meredith safe from harm?"

"No, Marvin's 'is mate," said Frank, nodding at Bronk "I'm Frank," he shook the outstretched hand "I'm security chief."

"No, I'm Marvin Calderwood," said the bewildered engineer, extricating his throbbing fingers from Frank's vice-like grip.

"Mr. Bronk is my assistant. I was just…"

"Make up your mind," said Frank, shaking his head, "don't you even know who you are?" He raised an eyebrow at Bronk and laughed. "Ha! And people say I'm stupid."

"Never mind that, Marvin," said Bronk, forestalling any further confusion, "we have to act quickly. Frank, I assume you have merely incapacitated our guest?"

"Huh?" Frank scowled, "In cap what? Why can't you speak fucking English?"

"I say, there's no need for that sort of language, young man!" Marvin bristled, "We must always keep our decorum, even in desperate circumstances, it's what separates us from the animals."

"Hahaha! Oh fuck off," replied Frank. "Guns, motors and money, that's what makes us better than animals. I'd like to see a bloody panda rip the ignition out of a Renault Clio and bypass the alarm in eleven seconds, then drive getaway for an armed robbery. Fucking decorum. Jesus Christ, Bronk, who is this bloke."

Marvin just stared in astonishment, stunned into silence by Frank's outburst and Bronk only just managed to stifle a laugh at the offended expression on his face. "Frank, I just wanted to make sure you hadn't killed Mr. Forrester, that's all."

"Killed 'im? Nah, if I'd meant to top the sod, I'd 'ave made sure of it back there," he indicated the now smooth disc of the wormhole, hovering silently behind them, "but I figured you needed 'im alive."

"Thank you Frank, that was very thoughtful of you."

Frank cracked his knuckles, grimacing as he remembered too late about his broken fingers, then said, reciting as if by heart, "I am an expert in all forms of pac-if-ic-ation and forcible restraint, specialising in security and close protection details." He grinned proudly at Bronk, "What d'you reckon?"

"That's great Frank," Bronk had been giving Frank some tips on promoting himself as a freelance security specialist and the reformed thug seemed to have been doing his homework, "but right now, we need to get

Forrester out and about, before the morning rush hour."

"What exactly do you intend to do with this villain?" asked Marvin, poking Forrester, who was now noisily snoring with his face pressed against the cold stone floor, with the toe of his boot.

"How do you know this plan of yours is even going to work? My family may be in danger if his men are still holding them hostage."

"I think your family is fine, Marvin, they already released them, remember?" Bronk tried to reassure his old friend.

"They won't waste time going after them again. Forrester was more interested in stopping us from undermining the foundations of his empire to worry about them anyway."

Paul Forrester chose that moment to stir from his Frank-assisted nap, groaned loudly and attempted to raise his head. Marvin jumped back and pointed a trembling finger at the sprawled figure. "Quick, stop him! He's trying to escape!."

"There you go again," said Frank calmly, reaching down and grabbing a handful of Forrester's hair, "getting your bollocks knotted for no reason." He lifted Forrester's head slightly and then, with what appeared to be some precision, tapped it sharply on the floor, whereupon, Forrester collapsed once more.

Bronk winced.

"Thank you Frank, what would we do without your expertise? Now, it's time for the star of the show to make his grand entrance."

He turned to Marvin, who was looking from one of them to the other, seemingly at a loss for words.

"Marvin, you can remain here and monitor the rift; we don't want any nasty surprises." he handed his friend the pepperpot pistol, "Anyone, apart from a well spoken but possibly rather angry young woman with blond hair comes through the portal; shoot them, ok?"

Marvin swallowed, puffed up his chest and nervously took the gun. "You can rely on me, Bronk," he clapped his faithful assistant on the shoulder, "you do what you have to do and I'll hold the fort here, never fear."

"Thank you, old friend, we'll be back as soon as we can, I promise." Bronk looked at Frank and nodded, then they both bent to pick up Forrester's limp form, draped his arms over their shoulders and made for the steps that led out onto the street.

The sound of the rain was audible for a second, then the door slammed shut and Marvin Calderwood was alone in his lab, with only the hypnotically rippling silver disc for company.

From her vantage point, high on the branch of a tree in the woods, two hundred years and a world away, Hannah also kept watch and waited.

And waited.

21
The Gang's All Here

Hannah Hannah looked down through a gap in the leaves of the lower canopy. From her position on the branch of an ancient, spreading oak tree she could see quite a distance from her dizzying perch twenty feet above the ground. She had clambered up here after Frank had rugby tackled Forrester and carried him through the rift and now had a good view of the clearing and the few remaining searchers, who roamed unenthusiastically around the woods below.

Two of Forrester's protection detail were stationed at the rift, keeping a wary eye on it whilst staying a safe distance away and making aimless circuits of the clearing, peering into the gloomy dawn light which filtered down through the branches of the trees, occasionally talking quietly on their radios.

She looked at her watch. It was nearly an hour since Frank and Forrester had disappeared and now she was getting a cramp in her thigh. Hannah eased her frozen, numb backside off the branch and lowered her feet onto the one beneath her, carefully locating hand-holds before stretching her stiff legs and continuing her descent. I can't just perch in a tree and wait, she thought, I have to get to the rift, I've got to…

Then she slipped.

It was lucky for her that she passed between the two lowest branches, giving her a clear, uninterrupted fall of about eight feet to a relatively soft landing on the leafy woodland floor.

Not quite so fortunate for one of Forrester's men, who

chose that particular moment to wander past and had stopped to relieve himself against the trunk of the oak.

"Ooooh, Shhiiiiitt..!" was the last thing the hapless henchman heard, before he looked up and caught a pair of size seven, sensible brown walking boots full in the face, propelled by the weight of the rapidly accelerating Hannah, who crashed to the ground and rolled to a stop against a tree stump.

She paused to regain her breath and check for broken bones, then looked around, expecting any minute that hordes of armed thugs were going to arrive and drag her off to the villains' dungeon. Or wherever your modern evil criminal mastermind takes his victims nowadays. She was new to all this intrigue and derring-do and wasn't up on the etiquette, but she had seen a lot of Hollywood conspiracy thrillers and she was sure that by this point, Mel Gibson or Bruce Willis would already have made a bow and arrow out of twigs and deadly tree frog venom, but all she had was... Hannah suddenly had an idea.

Hurrying over to the fallen goon, she tried not to look too closely at the peculiar angle of his neck or the glassy, staring eyes or even the comical look of surprise on his face and quickly searched his pockets.

She found his gun and a small radio, then crept as silently as she could towards the gleaming silver disc, crawling from tree to tree until she was at the edge of the clearing, taking care not to be seen by the guards who were standing together smoking nervously, casting suspicious glances at the rift and chatting quietly.

She jumped as a sudden, loud crackling noise came from her coat pocket and a distorted voice said; "Team number 2, report.....Come in Team 2..." She scrabbled frantically to reach the radio, cursing her stupidity for not turning down the volume, then looked up as she heard a shout from the guards who had spotted her and were coming her way, drawing their weapons and looking very pissed off indeed.

"Shit, shit, shit, shit, SHIT!" said Hannah.

"Ok then. Come in Team number 2, your time is up!"

With that, she rose from her hiding place and ran as fast as she could towards the shimmering portal, hanging there in the first hazy rays of sunshine like an enchanted mirror from a fairy tale.

"Hey, stop right there!" one of the guards yelled at her, "Stop, or I'll shoot!"

"No! Fucking! Chance!" Hannah's only other reply was to raise her liberated pistol and empty the magazine in their general direction as she ran.

Unsurprisingly, none of her shots connected, although one did actually vanish with a PFITZZ! into the shining portal, leaving a brief ripple and nothing else, but her barrage did serve to slow them down long enough for her to reach her goal.

Barely breaking step and purely as a last minute reflex, Hannah bent down and scooped up the two wired together phones in the second before sheer momentum took her through the rift. She saw the bottom edge of the circular portal twist up and in on itself, then she was swallowed by the spiralling, iridescent glow of the wormhole corridor and she passed out.

Marvin Calderwood pulled out his pocket watch and looked at it for the tenth time in as many minutes. Where in God's name had they got to?

Bronk and that hooligan, Frank, had left with Forrester over an hour ago and the grey light of morning was already filtering through the small grubby windows of his basement laboratory, situated at ceiling height and giving a view of the first hurrying feet of the day as their owners headed off to work, and now Marvin was getting nervous.

He was just trying to decide whether he should risk

leaving his post as guardian of the portal to go looking for them, when there was a noise like a swarm of angry wasps, a small spot on the surface of the rift erupted briefly and one of the glass flasks on his desk exploded into fragments.

"What the..?!" Marvin threw himself flat on the floor behind the generator console, grabbing the revolver from his pocket as he did so.

There was silence for a moment, then the familiar crackling, fizzing sound and burning ozone smell of someone materialising through the rift filled the room, then more silence.

Marvin waited. When no other sounds had come from the other side for a full minute, he finally plucked up the courage to peek around the corner of the console. "Oh my goodness!"

Marvin stood and quickly went to where Hannah's dirty and disheveled figure was sprawled on the cold slabs. A nasty gash on her forehead evidence of her uncontrolled arrival on the laboratory's stone floor.

Hannah groaned and her eyelids fluttered open, squinting against the arc lamps that still burned around the room. Marvin reached for a mug of water on his desk and, lifting her head gently, he trickled a few drops into her mouth, "Here, drink this," he said, "don't try to move, just lay there a moment and catch your breath." Hannah nodded gratefully, swallowed the first mouthful and coughed, then her hands felt for the mug and she took it, draining the rest in one go.

After slowly dragging herself into a sitting position, with Marvin hovering around her like a mother hen, clearly not sure whether to assist her and risk causing offence, or make discretion the better part of valour and keep his hands to himself, she put down the mug and wiped an arm across her face, then looked up and smiled wearily.

"You must be Marvin, it's good to finally meet you." She tried in vain to stand up, slumped back to the floor and shrugged apologetically. "I don't suppose you'd give me a hand up would you, my legs seem to have gone on strike?"

"Oh my dear lady, I'm most terribly sorry," said Marvin, "where are my manners?" He pulled a chair from under the desk and helped Hannah onto it. "There. Now, is there anything I can get you? A little brandy perhaps?"

"It's a tempting offer, Marvin, really it is," she said, "but I think we should keep our heads clear for now, don't you?" Hannah cautiously made another attempt at standing upright, swaying gently as she clung to the back of the chair, while Marvin looked on with a frown of concern.

"Right," she said, after the dizziness and nausea from the trip through the rift had sufficiently faded, "I suppose we had better go and find what sort of trouble our two partners in crime have got themselves…"

She didn't get any further, because at that moment the door to the street opened and the sound of footsteps made them both turn, to see Bronk and Frank coming down the steps into the lab

"Ah, Miss Meredith," grinned Bronk, "so good of you to join us. Just in time to see our plan reach its conclusion."

22
Out of the Comfort Zone

Images of… lights, streaming past in rapidly strobing patterns; tumbling head over heels through the disorienting, formless glow. Then struggling, wrestling with an unseen assailant, impact on hard stone and a desperate fight, then, nothing...

Paul Forrester groaned and rolled over, feeling the rough texture of wooden boards against his cheek; the images in his head faded as consciousness slowly returned and he became aware of the sounds and smells around him. He sat up, wincing at the stiffness in his muscles, seized up from lying out in the cold, damp air of early morning and bruised from his fight with Frank, then, and only then, did he open his eyes and take in his surroundings.

He was on the back of a large wooden cart, a tarpaulin covering one end, from under which he had a narrow view of what seemed to be a deserted alley. The cart was about thirty feet from where the alley joined a busy road. Forrester could see figures hurrying past and hear the sound of voices, one man's voice, in particular, was raised above the others, repeating the same phrase over and over, though he couldn't make out what he was saying.

He crawled out from under the cover and, holding onto the side of the cart for support, he heaved himself upright. Taking a few shaky steps backwards and forwards, he stretched his legs and waiting for the blood to start circulating again. Once he felt steady enough, he jumped down onto the filthy cobbles and cautiously approached the mouth of the alley.

Getting closer to the road, the repetitive, unintelligible voice resolved itself into words and as Forrester reached the pavement and looked out onto the bustling street, he realised it was the shouted advertisement of a man selling newspapers.

"Read all about it, read all about it! Escaped villain on the loose. Wanted for kidnapping and murder! Read all about it, read all about it…"

A woman stopped in front of the newsstand and dug in her bag until she seemed to find what she wanted, handed over a coin and took a paper from the stack.

"Ta, luv," said the vendor, "terrible what the upper classes get up to, ain't it? Murder and kidnapping, that's what they say they're after this Forrester character for. Look at his picture, that's pure evil in that stare, you mark my words; 'e's as guilty as sin, no matter what they say 'e done."

Forrester froze, then shrunk back into the shadows of the alley, panicky thoughts chasing themselves around his head. The man had said his name, there was no doubt about that, but… that didn't make any sense. The police had never been a problem for him before, he'd always just paid them off and anyway, he was personal friends with the Chief Constable and on the board of the golf club committee with the local commissioner, they would have certainly tipped him the wink if anything untoward was on the cards, besides…

"What the fuck..?" Directly opposite him, pasted on the door of the shop adjacent to the alley, was a poster displaying a rough but recognisable likeness of Forrester, beneath the words WANTED: REWARD, scrawled in black ink, the letters blurred from the night's rain but still readable.

He glanced around, checking he wasn't being watched, then darted across the narrow alley and tore down the thin sheet of paper, stuffing it into his coat pocket. He retreated to where the cart was parked and was clambering back into the safety of the covered section, to properly study the shocking poster when a voice from behind froze him in the act.

"That's far enough, sir, please keep your hands where I can see them and step down from there."

Forrester sighed, stepped back down from the cart and turned to meet his fate...

23

Predator becomes the Prey

It had taken a moment for Forrester to put his finger on what was different. When he'd first come round on the back of the cart, the realisation he had actually travelled in time only sank in when he'd seen with a shock that everyone was in period costume.

Well, he corrected himself, not costume, of course, it was just what they wore here (now), but it was one thing in particular which drew his attention to all the other differences. The lack of motorised traffic noise, the air was filled with sound, but not in the same way as the London he knew, the background noises were more human, somehow.

And the smell; a mixture of soot, horse manure, sewage, and rotting vegetables, it assaulted the senses like a blunt instrument, battering his nostrils into submission and forcing Forrester to breathe through his mouth. That, or risk passing out from the overpowering stench. Once he overcame his initial nausea, only to find he was a wanted fugitive and as if that wasn't bad enough, here he was faced with another irritating minion. And such a polite one, too.

"That's far enough, sir, please keep your hands where I can see them and step down from there."

Forrester turned to find a rather nervous looking young man, in an oversize belted greatcoat and high, domed helmet with a silver badge on it, one hand holding a small wooden truncheon in a vaguely threatening manner.

"Could you tell me what you're doing, climbing into Mr. Grainger's delivery cart?" The young policeman was obviously making an effort to project authority, but he wasn't fooling Forrester, who immediately dismissed him as no threat and advanced on him, smiling and opening his arms in a friendly gesture.

"My good man, there's clearly some misunderstanding here," still smiling, Forrester reached casually into his coat, "allow me to give you my card…"

The constable looked uncertain and opened his mouth to say something, but now Forrester was in front of him, whipping his hand out far too quickly to be giving him his card and he just had time to see the glint of a blade as Forrester viciously lashed out with it and jammed it into his throat.

The young man made a horrible gurgling noise as blood erupted from his mouth and clutched at the place where Forrester's knife was sticking out of his neck, staggered back a few paces and fell to his knees, his eyes staring at his attacker in confusion for a few seconds before falling forward into the gutter and lying still.

Forrester looked toward the mouth of the alley to check nobody had seen him then bent to retrieve the knife, pulling it out and wiping the blade on the constable's coat. Only then did he head down the alley, away from the bustle of the main road, eventually reaching a dead end and clambering over a wall to find himself in some kind of walled kitchen garden with greenhouses and vegetable beds arranged in a neat grid pattern, fruit trees growing at one end.

There was a recessed doorway in the thick stone wall on his left and Forrester hurried along the path until he reached the heavy oak and iron door. Cautiously trying the latch and finding it unlocked, he eased the door open and peered through the gap. Seeing nobody in the yard beyond, Forrester slipped through and quietly closed the door behind him.

He looked around, taking in the small outbuildings and

gardening implements with a glance, then noticed a sign on another door in the wall opposite and moved closer until he could read the gothic lettering, Zoological Society of London. Botanical garden – PRIVATE – AUTHORISED ENTRY ONLY

So, thought Forrester, at least I know where I am now, Regent's Park, where London Zoo will be. It was originally a private collection, he knew, dedicated purely to scientific study, until the Society was eventually forced to open the gates for paying customers, to raise the funds necessary for its upkeep.

Forrester had evidently been transported back to a time before the great unwashed British public had been allowed to roam freely amongst the newly discovered wonders of the animal kingdom, so the chances of him encountering anyone wandering around the grounds were slim.

Nevertheless, before seeing what was on the other side of the door, he looked through the assortment of tools in the yard until he found a short, heavy hammer. A knife was all very well, but it was so messy. Dropping the hammer into his coat pocket, he stepped through the door into a dark, arched corridor between two buildings with the only light coming through an ornate iron gate at the far end. Seeing no other exits from the yard, Forrester shrugged, closed the door and headed for the gate.

He was almost at the end of the tunnel when he heard the sound of a whistle somewhere behind him and its relevance wasn't lost on him. Like a bloody police siren, he thought. They found the dead copper. Damn!.

He hurried to the gate and felt for the latch, frantically searching for a way get it to open, when the light was suddenly blocked out and he looked up to see two figures filling the archway.

"It's him!"

"That's that Forrester bastard from the posters! He killed Jenkins, get him!"

One man began rattling at the gate, while his companion stood back and shouted up the street. "We've found him, he's at the back of the gardens!"

The sounds of running feet and more whistles came from the opposite end of the tunnel and Forrester turned to see the door opening and the silhouettes of several men, shoving each other out of the way in their eagerness to get to him first.

Then one of the men at the gate managed to get it unlocked and the screech of rusted hinges was the last thing Forrester heard before the first of many enthusiastic blows from several small but surprisingly effective wooden truncheons rendered him unconscious.

24
Street Life

Marvin Marvin Calderwood stood back and looked at his three fellow collaborators with a thoughtful expression. "I think you should pass all but the most rigorous of inspections," he said, frowning slightly as if there was something he couldn't quite put his finger on. "Ummm, Frank, could I ask, are you supposed to be a travelling musician, because I'm not sure that suit is quite right...?"

"You talkin' to me?" scowled Frank.

"I told you, we should all be using our code names, to get into character, kind of fing. You know, like them actors what walk around in costume at home, make 'em feel like someone else, right?"

Marvin sighed. He had just suggested that maybe he could find them some less conspicuous clothing so that they could mingle unnoticed in public and hopefully ensure Forrester didn't manage to escape the trap they had laid for him.

But once Frank got the bit between his teeth, it was hard to divert him from the course he had chosen and ever since his promotion to "security chief", it was apparent that he considered every aspect of anything even vaguely "operational" to be his responsibility.

So he'd insisted on them all having cover names, despite the fact they'd be just as anonymous as themselves and had made them refer to each other using only these names for the last two hours so there would be no "Great Escape slip-ups", as Frank put it.

"Ok Frank," said Marvin. Seeing Frank's glare, he hurriedly checked a sheet of paper on his desk."Sorry, I mean, Mr. Corleone…did I say something amusing, Hannah?"

"No, no, don't mind me," Hannah managed to say, suppressing the urge to giggle, "just clearing my throat, it's fine, really."

"Right, in that case, we'd better get going," said Bronk, shrugging into his coat, "I think Mr. Forrester should have awoken from his nap by now."

"Oi, what d'you fink you're doing in that coat, that ain't orfentic is it?" said Frank.

"I think you'll find Mr. Bronk's…excuse me," Marvin consulted the paper again, "Mr. Dahmer's coat is actually as authentic as it gets, Fra…Mr. Corleone, sir," he smiled nervously, "as it is the very one I bought him only two Christmases ago. Since then, it has been somewhat out of time, so to speak."

"Some things never go out of style," said Bronk, "a good coat will last you a lifetime…" he appeared to consider this, then said with a grin, "sometimes even two."

"I still don't understand the violin case," said Marvin, "what if somebody asks you to play for them?"

"Oh for fuck's sake," grumbled Francis 'Sonny' Corleone, to give him his new full name. "Fine, forget the bloody violin case! Honestly, subtlety is lost on some people."

"Never mind, Frank," said Hannah, smiling sweetly in the face of Frank's scowl, "I'm sure the population of Victorian London will appreciate the dedication to your oeuvre."

Frank frowned suspiciously; he was sure "oeuvre" had something to do with eggs but didn't want to look stupid, so he let it go. Besides, he'd gotten to be quite fond of Hannah, (although he'd rip your arms off and feed them to you if you even thought of telling her that) she'd proven she could look after herself and she wasn't a whiny bitch when she had to get her hands dirty, which made her ok by

Frank.

Having satisfied their head of security they were "mission ready", the three of them finally left Marvin to recalibrate the generators for their journey home and headed up the basement stairs. The door at the top opened onto an alleyway behind the nondescript red brick building which housed the laboratory, the bustling main thoroughfare of Primrose Hill visible only a few yards away.

Despite Hannah's initial apprehension, the trio raised no eyebrows amongst the members of the public. Neither shopkeepers or tradesmen who thronged the street, nobody paid them the slightest attention, except for one small boy who bumped into Frank, took one look at his permanent lopsided scowl and burst into terrified floods of tears.

The child's mother turned in horror at the sound of her bawling offspring and, following the direction of his shaking finger, looked up at the, admittedly unnerving sight of Frank, trying his best to smile disarmingly. At that moment, she obviously decided being a good parent warranted more in the way of discretion and less in the way of valour, favoured Frank with a scowl of her own and, sweeping the still crying boy into her arms, she hurried away.

"What?" asked Frank, with apparent bewilderment, "What did I do?"

"I think it's just your resting bitch face," said Hannah, innocently, "don't take it personally."

"Hey, who're you calling a bitch?" bristled the newly incarnated Mr. Corleone, "There's no need to be personal, just coz I got a unique bone structure."

"I believe Hannah is referring to your features not being overly demonstrative of your sunny emotional disposition, Frank, she wasn't insulting your masculinity," said Bronk, with an admirably straight face, "don't take it personally."

"There you go again," Frank growled, "using ten words when one will do, why do you 'ave to be such a smartass?"

"Boys, boys, we really must get going," interrupted Hannah, "where did you say you left Forrester?"

"We took him over the canal and left him in an alley near Regent's Park," Bronk replied, "if we walk just a little further, we'll come to the footbridge."

As they made their way down the busy street, Hannah had to fight the urge to stop and gaze at the shop displays and marvel at the whole... Victorian-ness of everything. She had to keep reminding herself that they were actually here, or rather, now, and not in some elaborate theme park. After a while, she just tried not to think about it, because the very idea of it still made her head hurt.

Hannah was jolted from her reverie by the sound of high pitched whistles coming from some way in front of them, followed by the sound of running feet from the opposite direction. A disturbance on the pavement behind them made her turn, only just giving her time to avoid being trampled by three burly policemen who were shouldering their way through the crowd, prodding those slowest to move with the ends of their stubby truncheons, clearly not in the mood to be obstructed in their duty.

Bronk steadied Hannah as she stumbled out of the way, holding onto her as the men rushed past, while Frank stood and sneered at their retreating backs.

"Ha! Fuckin' hell, what are they wearing?" he bellowed, in what Frank, method actor, probably thought of as his best sotto voce.

"They wouldn't last five minutes back home, looking like that. No stab vest or fuck all, and that little wooden stick? Nah, they'd be fucked, no two ways about it."

"Yes, thank you Francis, for that fashion critique," said Bronk, glancing around to see if Mr. Corleone's outburst had drawn any unwanted attention. "I think it might be unwise to antagonize the local law enforcement unless it becomes absolutely necessary… " seeing Frank's expression, Bronk hurriedly translated. "Don't take the piss out of the coppers' stupid costumes, Frank, we don't need the aggro."

Frank shrugged. "Fair enough, Jeffrey," he said with a broad wink, "you could have just said so."

Bronk rolled his eyes. "Come on, let's see what all the excitement's about." Grabbing Hannah's hand, he dived into the crowd, following in the wake of the policemen.

Two minutes later they found themselves on the towpath of the Grand Union Canal. A string of barges, carrying loads of coal and what looked like bales of cloth were being drawn steadily along by pairs of horses which plodded past, seemingly oblivious to the noise of shouting and loud whistles, coming from just over the bridge on the canal, not far from where they stood.

The first of the barges were just passing beneath the bridge as the three of them ran across it, hearing the excited shouting grow louder and more aggressive, then suddenly cease, to be replaced by a ragged cheer and more excitable shouting when they reached the other side. They followed the noise until they turned a corner and spotted a group of uniformed men emerging from an arched gateway, carrying a bundled tarpaulin, containing what looked like a body.

Waiting in the road was a black painted, horse-drawn wagon with Pentonville written on the side, beneath a royal crest, with only a small barred window in the rear door to allow in light. One of the infamous "Black Maria" wagons, which toured the streets of Victorian London, collecting unfortunate miscreants and carting them off to the newly built Pentonville prison, many of whom would never be seen again.

One of the men carrying the bundle casually dropped his end of it so he could open the door as they approached the back of the wagon, and the tarpaulin fell away, revealing Paul Forrester's bruised and bleeding face. Hannah heard his head bump loudly on the step as it fell towards a second, sharper impact on the cobbles of the road.

Once the policeman had the door open, they heaved Forrester's limp form into the darkened interior and slammed the door shut. Slapping a hand on the side as a signal to the driver, who flicked his reins over the backs of the horses and the wagon trundled off up the street.

"So, everything seems to be going to plan," said Bronk, turning to Hannah and Frank, "and I believe I promised to buy you both lunch." He looked theatrically at his watch. "A couple of days ago, in fact. Well, Marvin was good enough to provide me with some money for expenses, so what do you say I treat you to a nice plate of jellied eels?"

Frank's resting bitch face split into a wide grin, "Now you're talking, let's eat!"

"Oh, you have to be kidding me! People don't actually eat this stuff, do they?" Hannah looked at the bowl of jellied eels Frank handed her with disgust, "I'm not all that hungry, now that I come to think about it."

"Don't knock it until you've tried it, that's what my old mum used to say." Frank grinned and shoveled a huge fork full of the vile grey mess into his mouth.

"It really isn't as bad as it looks," said Bronk, dipping a lump of bread into his bowl and eating it with apparent relish, "once you get used to it."

"Ok, I'm holding you to that," Hannah promised, looking down at her bowl with deep suspicion, "although I don't plan on getting too used to it."

She tore a chunk off the loaf Bronk offered her and scooped up as much of the fishy gunk as she dared, took a deep breath and nibbled the smallest possible bite from the end.

"Um, Frank," said Bronk, "I think perhaps you'd better get out of the way, I think Hannah needs to… Ah, too late."

Frank looked down at his shoes with distaste, "They were nice shoes them, too," he said, "still, could've been worse I suppose." He peered around the side of the jellied eel stall with an amused expression, from where they could still hear Hannah violently throwing up.

25
Case Study

Detective Chief Inspector Philip Ryland turned from watching the last streaks of sunset red fading from the sky outside his window, looked once more at the teetering pile of case files on his desk and sighed. There seemed to be some sort of mini crimewave going on at the moment and he couldn't help thinking it had something to do with the lead story in the evening paper:

"MILLIONAIRE BUSINESSMAN VANISHES: STOCK MARKET IN TURMOIL!!" screamed the headline of the tabloid on his desk, alongside a photo of a busty, half-naked glamour model and the inevitable, non-ironic sidebar rant about evil immigrants, who were apparently stealing our jobs, whilst simultaneously being lazy benefit scroungers.

In addition to the file, Ryland had been reading about a shooting out in the sticks on Friday, a farmhouse peppered with bullet holes, with considerable amounts of blood found at the scene, although a body had yet to be recovered. There were also numerous reports of other disturbances, all occurring in the last three days, all seeming to indicate a series of events with one common denominator; a certain Paul Forrester.

DCI Ryland mentally ticked off the facts as he knew them:

– Two cars, one with its tyres shot out, found outside a cottage owned by this Meredith woman, now also considered a missing person, who had disappeared along with her car from the shot-up farmhouse. The second found abandoned in some woods a few miles away, both registered to companies owned by Forrester.

– Then, a break-in at a private school early Saturday morning had triggered a silent alarm. When local officers had investigated, the body of a man with head injuries was found and yet another vehicle was discovered, also traced back to one of Forrester's labyrinthine corporate accounts.

– A member of the public had reported hearing gunshots at a truck stop diner, a couple of hours after the local police arrived at the school and since he was nearby, the senior officer despatched a car from the school to check it out. When they arrived, the manageress of the diner claimed ignorance of any disturbance and, with no crime to investigate, they had taken it no further.

– He was still waiting to hear what else his men had found in the woods where one of the cars had been found. There were already unconfirmed reports coming in of further bodies at the scene and he was sure a connection to Forrester would soon turn up.

– And now this, the disappearance of the man himself. Nobody had seen or heard anything of Forrester since he left his office on Friday evening and, although the official line from the company was that he was out of the country on business, Ryland couldn't help thinking more was going on than he was being told. And if there was one thing Philip Ryland didn't like, it was being kept in the dark.

He looked up in irritation as a loud burst of laughter from outside his office broke his train of thought and was about to go and tell the detectives on duty to keep the noise down when he remembered the squad was having a few birthday drinks for the retired ex-custody officer. Sergeant Howell was turning 75 today but still came in occasionally to do the odd bit of paperwork when the station was short staffed.

Ryland took off his glasses and rubbed his eyes. Maybe a couple of drinks and taking a break from the case would give him some inspiration. He closed the file, placed it, along with the newspaper on top of the precarious stack and went in search of some scotch.

Meanwhile, thirty miles north and a hundred and fifty years in the past, the elusive Mr. Forrester was being introduced to his new accommodation.

"Oooh, look at the gentleman," said a voice with knuckle-dusters in it, from out of the shadows, "aren't we the lucky ones, to share a cell with the aristocracy, no less."

There was laughter from the other inhabitants of the dimly lit, foul smelling room in which Forrester had awakened a few minutes before. A motley collection of filthy and unfriendly looking thugs who sat against the walls, leering down at him as he lay in the centre of the floor, his face pressed into the rotting straw that covered the stone slabs.

"Yeah, what did the Peelers get you for then, your lordship?"

"Did you run someone over with your carriage?"

"Get your maid up the duff, did you?"

More laughter, followed by the sound of someone loudly clearing their throat and spitting.

Forrester felt a glob of something slimy land on his cheek and lifting his hand to wipe it off, he slowly rose to a sitting position and looked around the dingy cell. A large, red faced man stared defiantly back at him from his seat on an upturned bucket, his expression daring Forrester to object, the men on either side of him grinning in anticipation of whatever came next.

However, before any of them had a chance to react, Forrester was on his feet. He took two quick strides and kicked the bucket out from under the man, at the same time jabbing upwards into his windpipe with stiffened fingers. The thug clutched at his throat and collapsed with a choking noise, just as the slowest on the uptake of his henchmen made a move to stand up. His nose met Forrester's fist coming the other way and exploded with a gush of blood before he was on his feet. He screamed and fell back against the wall. The second of Red Face's companions wisely decided to make no further attempt to engage the crazy aristocrat and suddenly found something fascinating to stare at on the opposite wall instead.

Forrester glanced around at the remaining prisoners and, after seeing no other threats to his safety, retired to an empty corner of the cell to consider his predicament.

26
Paper Trail

Not unlike DCI Ryland, although with an arguably better grasp of the situation, Marvin Calderwood was poring over a desk covered in papers. The difference being, instead of trying to solve crimes, Marvin was trying to make sure they didn't happen in the first place.

Or, rather, weren't going to have happened... or maybe that should be wouldn't be about to have been going to happen... or something like that anyway, thought Marvin, who'd given up on tense conjugation a long time ago.

He studied the list of men's names on the sheet of paper in his hand, cross referencing them with a page in the ledger laid open atop the cluttered surface of his desk. This one showing a list of huge corporations, giant multinationals which Marvin only knew as names in a ledger, but which anyone from Hannah's time would recognise as major players in global finance, information technology, manufacturing and politics.

Throughout his enforced dealings with Forrester, Marvin had kept scrupulous and secret records of all the unscrupulous and secret things the cabal of corrupt industrialists and politicians had been doing, in preparation for their bid for world domination. At the time he'd known the knowledge may become useful, and provide leverage against Forrester, especially after he kidnapped Marvin's family-to-be in the future, but he hadn't considered exactly how he would use it.

Bronk's plan had finally given him an opportunity to make use of this carefully documented record of his unwilling collaboration. Forrester's plan had been fiendishly simple, he would target specific innovations or industrial processes from the past. Which, unknown to the scientists and engineers who discovered them, would provoke seismic shifts in the history of global technological advancement. Having pinpointed his victims, Forrester forced Marvin to draw up authentic legal documents for each patent he wished to steal from its rightful owners and register it in Forrester's name.

The papers were left with a well-established law firm in London, with instructions that they should be stored permanently in the safe and only viewed by the authorised agent of their anonymous but high-paying client, whose identity would only ever be known to whoever was in control of the law firm at the time. The agents were, had been..? were going to be..? the descendants of the man Marvin recruited to his nefarious cause soon after Forrester had entrapped him, his valet, Gideon.

Gideon and his son, then five years old, had come to Marvin three and a half years ago and the old engineer had grown fond of the bright and cheerful young man and his child, which was what made it all the more difficult a decision to get them involved. The irony was that Marvin didn't have anyone else he could trust and he dare not just hire some cutthroat off the streets to entrust his destiny to, leaving him with no choice but to let his one faithful friend in on his terrible secret and hope he didn't think Marvin had lost his mind.

As it turned out, after his first reaction of shock and disbelief had passed, Gideon was more than happy to go along with his fantastic story and needed no further encouragement to take up Marvin's generous offer. Forrester had provided a fortune in gold to fund Marvin's continuing experiments on the wormhole generators, a tiny fraction of which would make Gideon a wealthy man for life because, whether he was truly able to comprehend the proposition or not, all he had to do for the money was occasionally check some papers in a lawyer's safe, whenever one of the names on Marvin's list rose to prominence in their chosen field or profession.

Should Gideon, his son, or any of their descendants discover that someone on the list was about to introduce a brand new innovation to the world, they would produce the dated and suitably annotated patents and claim credit for the invention or discovery on behalf of their mysterious employer, one Mr Paul Forrester.

In this way, Forrester and his cronies could plunder the work of the last century and a half of brilliant minds and dedicated pioneers, reaping the huge rewards of corporate greed and power, without having lifted a finger to earn it.

When Marvin had told Bronk that a scientist responsible for one of Forrester's stolen electrical patents had died in a carriage accident, Bronk had a flash of inspiration. He would pay the scientist's family for their silence and cooperation, then assume the dead man's identity and publicly challenge Forrester in court for plagiarizing his life's work.

Now that Forrester had got himself arrested for murder, things had changed somewhat, but Bronk still needed a way to bring the whole devious edifice of Forrester's megalomania crashing down around his ears and this seemed the best chance for them to do it. Which was why Bronk and his "wife", Hannah, were about to leave for Pentonville prison; to blacken the rascal's name still further and hasten his downfall.

"All set?" asked Bronk, smiling encouragingly at Hannah and patting the capacious pockets of his overcoat for the fifth time, checking he had the all-important paperwork.

"I think so," replied Hannah, "but I'll be bloody glad to get out of this ridiculous dress."

Bronk laughed, "You look every inch the Victorian

scientist's wife, my dear," offering her his arm, "shall we go?"

Hannah stuck her tongue out at him, but nevertheless she placed her arm through his, waved regally at Marvin and Frank and the two of them went up the steps and out onto the street.

27
J'accuse

Bronk and Hannah stood in front of the small door, set into the huge and forbidding gates of Pentonville prison, waiting for someone inside to respond to Bronk pulling the bell rope.

"What if they don't believe us?" asked Hannah nervously, "we might never get out of there."

"I think you may be giving Victorian agencies of law and order a little too much credit," Bronk replied, patting her arm reassuringly, "we've gotten used to a world where the powers that be can track us down anywhere, anytime, just by the electronic signature and physical paper trail we leave behind us. Our very existence can be read like an open book, by anybody who has access to a computer and the ability to manipulate the system."

He gestured around them at the soot covered buildings and horse-drawn carriages which clattered past on the cobbled road surface. "Fortunately for us, the era of mass surveillance is still a distant fantasy, a gentleman's word is worth a lot more these days," he fished the patent documents out of his pocket, "especially when backed up by the appropriate paperwork, along with the aforementioned gentleman's ability to lie through his teeth, of course." He grinned cheerfully at Hannah, then hammered on the Judas gate and shouted to whoever was on the other side. "Come on, we haven't got all day you know!"

A third, still smaller hatch opened in the door-within-a-door and a grubby, unshaven face filled the space. "Alright, alright, keep yer 'air on, fer gawd's sake!

Blimey, you're an impatient one ain't ya? Whoever yer after, they ain't going nowhere, I promise you that." The man laughed and then coughed wetly. He turned his head away and spat, wiping his mouth as he looked back at Bronk and finally asked, "Who're you 'ere to see, anyway?"

"We have come to see whoever is in charge," said Bronk, in a pompous and disdainful voice, "we have important information, concerning a dangerous criminal who was recently apprehended. It's vital that we see somebody in a position of authority as soon as possible."

He looked steadily back at the guard, who seemed to be processing this latest input from the world outside his head with some difficulty, leading Bronk to wonder whether they had inadvertently stumbled upon one of Frank's ancestors, through some kind of temporal anomaly.

But the message obviously managed to fire up a few passing neurons, because his expression suddenly cleared and he said, "Aaahhhh, you wanna see the guv'nor! Why didn't you just say so?"

They heard the sound of bolts being drawn and the small, iron bound gate opened. Bronk smiled encouragingly once more and stepped over the sill into the courtyard beyond, then turned to offer his hand to Hannah, seeing her safely over the threshold and back into possible danger.

Paul Forrester sat and stared at the chunk of stale bread and fuzzy-edged cheese on the wooden plate, then looked up into the eyes of the man who had placed it in front of him. It was the fallen ringleader of the cell's thug hierarchy, the one Forrester had knocked off his perch earlier. The man, with a vivid bruise showing across his throat, nodded grudgingly at Forrester and returned to his clan of troglodytes, keeping a close eye on the new arrival until his back was once again safely up against the opposite wall.

Forrester nodded back, picked up the bread and tore off a bite, which he chewed with as much appreciation as he could muster, whilst simultaneously eyeing the cheese with deep suspicion. He was just wondering if he could pull off some sleight of hand, to give the impression that he'd eaten it. After all, no matter how much of an evil, venal bastard he was, Paul Forrester had always liked to think he had impeccable manners and he didn't want to seem ungrateful even now, when he was saved the trouble by one of the slovenly, badly dressed guards, who were ambling down the dingy corridor calling out his name.

"Forrester! Paul Forrester!"

The guard stopped in front of the cell door and peered in through the open hatch. "There's someone wants to make your acquaintance, your lordship."

There was nervous laughter from the other side of the cell, followed by the various sub-species of henchmen Sshssuh-ing each other, before gazing innocently at the walls and ceiling when Forrester glanced their way.

He stiffly rose to his feet, picked up the plate and crossed the filthy stone floor to where his cellmates were congregated and handed it to their leader. "Thanks for dinner, gents, but I think that's my cue to bid you good day." He bowed politely and turned to see the door opening, and the guard looking cautiously past him into the cell, one hand clutching a small club, as if he expected a stampede.

Forrester looked back over his shoulder, then turned to his escort and smiled, "Oh, I don't think they'll be any trouble today, officer."

Bronk watched the warden closing the door as he left

the room, then turned to Hannah. "I think he's convinced. You did very well, my dear, just the right combination of vulnerability and outrage."

Hannah grinned and let out a shaky breath. "I must say, I quite enjoyed it after a while. It's nice to be spoken to like a lady for a change, even if it was in a rather condescending way. He did seem to believe us though, didn't he? With any luck, they'll throw the book at him."

The door opened and the warden returned, accompanied by two scruffy looking guards, who stood either side of the doorway and waited. After a moment, there was the sound of footsteps outside in the corridor and a third guard arrived, stepped into the room and looked to the warden for instructions, who in turn spoke to Bronk. "Right, Sir, if you'd like to…" Hannah coughed.

"Please, do excuse me; Sir and Madam, if you would like to remain seated, we shall bring in the prisoner under guard and you can tell us if you recognise him." He looked uncertainly at Hannah. "Um, if you would feel safer…"

The warden caught Hannah's look, Bronk reckoned he should think himself lucky he didn't burst into flames on the spot, then wisely addressed the guard. "Bring in the prisoner."

The guard left the room and returned a few seconds later with a somewhat battered and grimy figure in a torn and bloodstained suit, who Hannah nevertheless immediately identified as the man responsible for turning her life upside down. "That's him!" she cried, pointing a trembling finger at Forrester's shocked face. "That's the man who tried to blackmail my husband and stole his life's work, the scoundrel!"

28
Fate takes a Hand

Thinking about it later, Hannah realised they should have been ready for trouble as soon as Paul Forrester walked into the room. After all, here they were in a world that, despite being superficially less "civilised" than the one they were used to, was far less accustomed to the kind of casual brutality some people were capable of, especially from someone as apparently upper class as their prisoner. Forrester knew this and had no hesitation in using it to his advantage.

Before the warden or either of his men had time to react to Hannah's dramatic accusation, Forrester suddenly turned and delivered a deadly accurate roundhouse punch to the head of the guard nearest him, connecting solidly with his temple and dropping the man like a poleaxed ox.

The second guard managed to shake himself free of his drunken torpor, just in time to catch a brief glimpse of Forrester's rapidly approaching face, before a vicious headbutt simultaneously broke his nose and slammed the back of his skull into the metal door frame, sending him sliding down the wall to join his comrade on the floor.

The warden looked down at the motionless bodies of his two men, up at Forrester's evil grin, then at Bronk and Hannah, who stood frozen, stunned by the sudden violence. He was just opening his mouth to say something to Hannah, when he saw her eyes widen and, too late, turned in the direction of her gaze.

He probably never even saw the guard's heavy club coming, as Forrester brought it down on his head with all the strength he could muster. The warden collapsed without a sound, a thin trickle of blood running from one ear, his eyes staring sightlessly at the ceiling.

Only now did Forrester seem to hesitate, glancing uncertainty from the open door to Bronk and Hannah and back again. He obviously came to a decision, shrugged and threw them a sardonic two-fingered salute, then turned on his heel and strode out of the room, closing the heavy door behind him.

Bronk rushed across the room and wrenched at the door handle, just as Forrester's grinning face appeared at the barred window and Hannah heard a click as the door was locked from the outside. Bronk pounded on the door in frustration, as Forrester pressed his face to the bars and finally broke the silence he'd maintained since arriving in the room just a few moments earlier.

He laughed mockingly and his eyes locked on Hannah's as he spoke. "I'm terribly sorry I can't stay and chat, Ms. Meredith, but I have a New World Order to organise. Mr. Bronk, I'd like to have had more time to question you about your treachery, but alas, I shall have to be content with abandoning the two of you to history and the mercy of Victorian justice." He laughed again. "Good luck explaining to the authorities how you came to be shut in a locked room with the warden's dead body, I'll be off now, cheerio."

And with that, Forrester disappeared from view, his hurrying footsteps fading until Hannah and Bronk were once more left in silence.

"Shit!" Hannah said, "Fuck, fuck, fuck, fuck!"

"Well, quite," replied Bronk, "I couldn't have put it better myself. Although, if you have anything of more practical nature to contribute, this would be a good time…" Bronk's voice trailed off as he started rifling through the drawers in the warden's desk.

Hannah looked like she might respond, then changed her mind and slumped into one of the hard wooden chairs.

"What exactly are you looking for?" she asked, watching Bronk emptying the contents of a drawer onto the desktop.

"Something thin and metallic," he said, "anything I could use to pick that lock."

"Like a hat pin, for instance?"

Bronk looked up from his frantic rummaging, "What?"

Hannah held up a long, wickedly sharp steel pin with a pearl top. "Marvin was very diligent when it came to making sure my costume was authentic. Is this the sort of thing you were after?"

Bronk was around the desk in three quick strides. He grabbed the hat pin, then bent and planted a kiss on Hannah's forehead. "You never cease to amaze me, my dear. Yes, this will suffice, I think."

Hannah actually blushed, much to her annoyance, covering her embarrassment by fussing with her hair.

Bronk chuckled to himself as he knelt in front of the door, then began to feel around inside the lock with the steel pin. He bent it this way and that, shaping the thin metal each time he inserted it, trying to match its profile to the pattern of tumblers inside the lock's primitive barrel mechanism.

Hannah watched Bronk work, anxiously wondering how long it would be before someone discovered the unconscious guards in the corridor and raised the alarm and she angrily scolded herself for letting Forrester get away again.

A coal merchant for the last thirty years, Duval J Hoath had just finished loading his wagon. He walked over to the gates of his yard and unlatched the padlock, pushing on the heavy timbers and feeling a twinge in his back that had been bothering him since last week.

The gate swung slowly open, emitting a low creak and Duval secured it to a stout stone post with a loop of rope.

He stretched his back, wincing at the crackling sensation, and he was repeating the same task with the second gate when a loud crash came from inside the yard, accompanied by the sound of one of his men shouting a warning. Duval Hoath rushed to the open gateway and was just in time to see the second half of his coal store, never the same since the fire a few weeks ago, collapse in a cloud of black dust and splintered wood.

This was one frightening noise too many for Hoath's usually docile horse and it chose that moment to get the hell out of there. With flaring nostrils and eyes rolling madly, the terrified animal strained against the weight of the wagon, jerking it sharply forward, which gave it just enough momentum for the next frightened pull to get the fully laden vehicle rolling across the yard and once moving, it accelerated rapidly.

Duval considered, for about a millisecond, trying to stop the runaway wagon as it exited his yard, then saw sense and dived out of the way at the last minute, narrowly escaping being crushed beneath the clattering wheels and landing heavily on the cobbles, not doing his back any favours in the process.

The horse now found itself trapped in the traces of an out of control coal wagon at the top of a hill with nobody on board to apply the brake and the vehicle was starting to pick up speed. So the unfortunate animal did the only thing its panicked brain could come up with, it started moving faster, so as not to get run over by its own wagon.

By the time the wagon reached the first junction, the horse was a rampaging, foam-flecked wreck and its legs were on the point of giving out anyway, even if some fool hadn't run straight out in front of it and put them both out of their misery.

"Aha!" Bronk jumped up from his crouching position

by the door and twisted the handle. The door swung open and he turned to Hannah. "Quickly! We may be able to catch up with him before he can reach the portal and escape."

Hannah stood and followed Bronk as he cautiously peered around the door, then slipped out into the corridor and back on the trail of the villainous Paul Forrester.

29
Sudden Death

Forrester hurried away from the warden's office, trusting his instincts to guide him in the right direction and trying to resist the temptation to run.

He ducked into a storeroom, to don the filthy uniform of one of the unconscious guards and stuffed his ruined coat behind a stack of crates, before locating a small door in the rough stone wall of the corridor and making his way down a narrow, winding stairway towards the basement. Following the revolting smells issuing from the kitchen, he found himself at a locked iron gate, through which he could see an open door that led out to a loading dock at the back of the prison.

Cursing his lack of foresight, Forrester was about to turn back and look for another way out, when he heard the sound of footsteps approaching from the direction he'd just come. He quickly considered his options and just as quickly realised he didn't have any, so he started patting his pockets in the manner of a man fruitlessly searching for something, all the while trying to gauge the distance between himself and the unseen threat behind him.

"Forgotten to collect them, have you?" The voice came from closer than he'd expected and Forrester tensed, gripping the short club he'd taken from the guard.

"You lot are all the same, you come down here once in a blue moon and forget you're supposed to sign out the service keys first" There was a metallic jangling noise as the man drew level with Forrester. "Here, out the way, I'll... Hey, who are you, I don't recognise..."

He didn't get any further; in one swift movement,

Forrester turned, already swinging the club as he came face to face with the guard, mouth open in surprise, arm coming up too late to prevent the blow that crashed down on the bridge of his nose. The man collapsed without a sound and Forrester immediately bent to retrieve the bunch of keys he had dropped, trying each in the lock until one turned with a click and the gate swung open.

Glancing back down the corridor to check nobody else was following, Paul Forrester relocked the gate and headed towards daylight and freedom once more.

Hannah and Bronk hadn't got more than a few yards from the warden's office, when they heard raised voices coming from ahead of them, closely followed by the sound of running feet. A second later they were confronted by the sight of half a dozen guards, some of them bleary-eyed and still pulling on their jackets, rushing around the corner towards them.

Bronk stopped, placing his hand on Hannah's arm as a warning not to go any further and positioning himself between her and the oncoming group of angry men. "Forrester, that damned murderer and kidnapper, he's escaped!" cried Bronk, waving frantically. "He locked my wife and I in the warden's office, after killing the poor man in front of our very eyes!"

He made a big show of his shock and outrage, turning to indicate Hannah, who had caught on quick and was doing her best sniveling, pathetic, damsel in distress routine let out a sob and blew her nose loudly into her lace handkerchief. "My wife had quite a turn, as you can see, she's in a state of shock."

He put a comforting arm around Hannah's shoulders as she obligingly wailed and clung to Bronk's arm, burying her face in the musty lapel of his ageless coat. "I must insist that we are escorted to the prison gates immediately, so that she may be allowed to recover from her ordeal in more…" he looked distastefully around him, "convivial surroundings."

One of the dumbstruck guards opened his mouth to reply and Bronk quickly went on. "I shall, of course, be available to provide whatever other assistance I can in catching the murderous swine. Once I have assured the safety of my wife and had a chance to catch my breath, I will return here in order to help in any way I can."

He stared expectantly at the man in front of him, who looked uncertain for a moment, then obviously decided Bronk and Hannah weren't worth his trouble and, in a broad Scottish accent, called back over his shoulder to one of the men at the rear of the little group, a rather timid looking individual, wearing cheap spectacles and trying to appear as inconspicuous as possible. "Mr. Barraclough, would you escort these good people to the main gatehouse, please. Be sure to get their names before they leave."

He nodded tersely to Bronk and touched the peak of his battered cap vaguely in Hannah's direction, then dismissed them with a wave of his hand and gestured to the remaining guards. "The rest of you, follow me!"

Just as soon as they had appeared, the guards were gone, leaving Hannah and Bronk in the suddenly silent corridor with Barraclough, who shuffled his feet nervously and mumbled, almost to himself. "Mr. Mackay said I should take you to the gate, sir. If you'd like to follow me…"

Five minutes later, Bronk and Hannah stepped through the small door in the main prison gate and let out a collective sigh of relief.

Hannah took a couple of deep breaths, waited until her heart rate had once again returned to a reasonable speed and looked at Bronk. "I don't know about you, but I could bloody well do with a drink."

Bronk was about to reply, when they heard a woman

scream, not far down the street from where they stood and a sudden disturbance in the crowd suggested they may not be as far behind Forrester as they thought.

"That's him!" The voice was clearly audible above the sounds of the busy street.

"Murderer! Get him, he killed a copper!"

Bronk looked at Hannah, then down the street, from where they could hear more angry shouting, then back at Hannah. "Go back to Marvin's place and lock the door, in case he heads there. I doubt he'll get far, though. I'll go after him, to make sure he's back in custody then I'll meet you there."

Hannah looked unsure, suddenly anxious at the thought of being on her own, but she told herself not to be so stupid and smiled at Bronk. "Be careful, you know what he's capable of." She leaned forward and kissed his cheek. "I wouldn't want anything to happen to you, after all we've been through together."

Bronk grinned, "You know me, I'm a survivor. Now, go!"

With that, he turned and ran toward the excited crowd and Hannah picked up the hem of her impractically long skirt and hurried after him. She needed to get to the main road to reach Marvin's lab and Bronk had vanished into the press of bodies before she got there.

Hannah made her way to the edge of the crowd where it was less dense and used her elbows, knees and pointed boots to carve a path through the rubber-neckers leaving a trail of scowling men, rubbing bruised ankles and winded stomachs, in her wake.

Forrester turned up the collar of his stolen jacket as he slipped out of the service entrance at the rear of the prison yard, glancing around him for any sign of police uniforms. Seeing none, he pulled the cap low over his eyes and headed toward the busy main road junction, some fifty yards down the street, hoping to lose himself in the bustling crowds until he could work out how to find Calderwood's laboratory and escape this godforsaken shithole, once and for all.

He was congratulating himself on his clean getaway, then that bloody woman screamed and he made the mistake of looking around at her, which was when she really started making a fucking nuisance of herself and drawing way too much unwanted attention his way.

He had to get the hell out of there right now, then worry about finding Marvin later, so he did the only thing there was left to do, he ran.

Bronk was almost free from the throng of jostling bodies when he caught sight of Forrester, sprinting down the pavement, pursued by a man in a striped apron, brandishing a meat cleaver, followed by two other shopkeepers and several laughing children, who dodged in and out of the crowd of people, carriages and horses with ease, yelling to each other as they watched the dramatic chase unfold.

He took off after Forrester, determined to bring him down now while he was still here, in the past, before he had a chance to continue his assault on the world of the future.

Before he could make good on his plan to take over the world.

Just for a few seconds, Bronk had his quarry in his sights. He was only ten yards behind Forrester as he ran across the main road and vanished into the crowds on the opposite pavement and he went straight after him.

Bronk's final thought as, too late, he noticed the shocked faces of the people at the kerb, was; "I wonder what they're all looking at…"

He turned…

…and just had time to register the sight of a speeding, terrified horse, propelled by an out of control, rapidly disintegrating coal wagon.

Then, nothing.

Hannah was, unfortunately, just in time to witness Bronk's spectacular and rather messy demise, after which she could have danced naked down the street and nobody would have noticed, such was the devastation and confusion caused by the crash.

So she made no effort to hide her grief; sobbing uncontrollably as she stumbled back to Marvin's house, bumping into people as her eyes blurred with tears for a man who she had known only a few days and yet who had saved her life countless times in that short time. She reached the rear of Marvin Calderwood's anonymous red brick house and hammered desperately on the door to the basement.

After a moment, Marvin opened the door and peered cautiously out, his frightened expression changing to one of concern when he saw Hannah's tear-streaked face, he stepped forward to steady her and her eyes rolled back in her head as she collapsed into his arms.

Looming faces… Stampeding, wild-eyed horses… Swirling lights… Screams… Dark, menacing corridors… Half-glimpsed, threatening figures… Panic…

Hannah jerked awake from the nightmare with a gasp, hair plastered to her scalp with sweat, flaking paint on the ceiling swimming into focus above her.

Her stomach suddenly heaved and she turned her head, retching dryly to one side of whatever she was lying on, then slowly, carefully, she swung her legs around and placed her feet on a cold stone floor. She was only just beginning to take in her surroundings when light flooded the room, accompanied by a familiar voice.

"Ah, you've decided to join us, 'ave you? About fucking time, too."

"Hello Frank," Hannah screwed up her eyes against the light, "nice to see you, too, I'm fine thanks."

There was an awkward pause. Well, as awkward as Frank ever got, anyway. He cleared his throat. "We 'eard about Mr. Bronk. I'm sorry, Hannah, I know you were kinda fond of 'im. You didn't ought to 'ave seen that, that's no sight for a lady." He paused, looking down at Hannah with something approaching respect. "No matter how tough they are."

Hannah stared up at Frank. She looked drained, eyes black ringed and devoid of emotion, skin pale and tight, jaws clenched rigidly together.

"We're going to take that fucker down, Frank." When she spoke, her voice was harsh and raw, her eyes locked on his.

"You and I, we are going to shut Paul fucking Forrester down for good and I know exactly how we're going to do it.

30
Calm before the Storm

Frank watched Hannah from across the room, as she spoke in a low but intense voice to Marvin Calderwood, occasionally jabbing the scattered pages of calculations and hurriedly sketched diagrams on the desk with her finger to enforce whatever point she was making. Although that was about the extent of what Frank could determine from his observations.

All this stuff about "temporal distortion", "event horizons" and "generator feedback loop optimisation" made about as much sense to him as… actually, now he came to think about it, albeit in the fairly limited way Frank thought about anything, it made just about as much fucking sense as anything else that had happened in the past week or so. In other words, no fucking sense whatsoever.

However, Frank had this advantage over, well, over pretty much everyone really, he had the ability to not think about stuff. He could not think about stuff so effectively, he'd been able to do, see, say, hear and, unfortunately, smell, countless truly horrible things in his professional life as a henchmen/independent security consultant, without it having the slightest effect on, for want of a better word, his sanity. Frank never had sweat-drenched, guilt-ridden nightmares, featuring the restless spirits of his victims, he slept like a baby.

Frank would see no contradiction in the fact he could coldly gun down an old lady who had somehow angered the man who paid his wages, then happily escort a similar old lady across the road half an hour later, even carrying her shopping to the bus stop for her.

So he had no problem at all, not thinking it strange, that he was sitting in the basement laboratory of a crazy Victorian scientist, waiting for some woman he didn't even know existed last week, to come up with a plan to stop a psychotic businessman take over the world using time travel and a gigantic global financial fraud. Nor did it concern him that he was about to once more surrender himself to an intangible, insubstantial, swirling tunnel of light in the interest of stopping the aforementioned psycho. And because none of these things would be improved or altered by the quantity or quality of thinking Frank could bring to the table, he patiently waited until someone else did all the mental heavy lifting and then applied the muscle and/or lethal intervention wherever directed. Which was just the way Frank liked things.

He had already helped Marvin secure the street door, as per Hannah's orders, making sure Forrester couldn't access the basement until they were ready for him and he'd been sitting here ever since, awaiting further instructions.

"Frank. Hello? Earth calling Frank." Hannah interrupted his non-thoughts, bringing him back to the here and now.

"I think we're about ready to try this, you need to get into position and hold on tight to the box of stuff."

She grinned humorlessly. Marvin had provided a square wooden box to hold the two interconnected phones and Hannah had thought it only proper to scrawl the word "Stuff" on the side. "When the rift opens we won't have long, we need to open and close it as quickly as possible if the plan has any chance of success."

Frank looked at her. "You're starting to sound like Bronk." He saw that dead, blank look in her eyes and hastily added, "Not that that's a bad thing, not saying it is, obviously, just that, well, you know… look, never mind,

I'll go and stand over there with the box, ok?"

Hannah didn't reply, instead, she turned to Marvin and gave him a brief hug and a peck on the cheek, making him blush like a schoolboy. "Now, Marvin, you will be sure to stick to the timetable, won't you? It's important that Forrester only comes through when we're ready."

"My dear lady," said the flustered, beetroot coloured scientist, "considering the terrible danger in which you are placing yourself, and the assistance you have rendered me thus far, both on my behalf and that of my family, this is the very least I can do. I assure you, I will lay down my life, if that is what's required of me, to ensure everything goes exactly according to plan."

Marvin straightened his shoulders and puffed out his chest, in imitation of what Hannah guessed was his idea of a man of action. "You can depend on me, Hannah, have no fear."

"Thank you Marvin, I'd never expected anything less from you, but if you follow the plan I don't think it will come to that. We'll speak again soon, I'm certain of it. Until then, look after yourself, it's been… interesting meeting you." Hannah turned to face the circle of arc lamps which stood at the far end of the lab, glanced at Frank, who stood obediently clutching the box of Stuff, then nodded at Marvin and heard the rising hum of the generators as he began the powering up sequence.

Two minutes later, Marvin watched the ripples on the ghostly, shimmering disc subside and slowly powered down the generators, then he was alone in the silent basement once more.

Now began the long wait, to see whether all their careful preparation would pay off, or if poor Bronk had died in vain.

31
Baiting the Trap

Ducking in and out of the throngs of people, most of whom were travelling in the opposite direction, drawn by the gory spectacle provided by Bronk's fortuitously terminal meeting with the runaway coal wagon. Forrester knew he had to find Marvin's laboratory but was more conscious of the need to find somewhere to lie low for an hour or two, just until the initial excitement around his escape had died down, then he would be free to track down Marvin and force the old fool to operate his infernal invention for the last time, allowing him to escape this nightmare and go home.

The thought of finally ridding himself of the thorn in his side that was Hannah bloody Meredith drove him on with a furious intensity that surprised even him. He never could have envisaged when he first attempted to buy that damn box from her, that she would cause him so much trouble and expense, otherwise he just would have killed her then and there and been done with it.

Well, that was it, no more mercy, no more chances. This time, when he caught up with her she was going to die, simple as that.

The subject of Forrester's frustrated rage and her loyal sidekick, the erstwhile Francis "Sonny" Corleone, were at that moment (within the very elastic definition of the term, considering the circumstances) setting in motion a plan they hoped would end this madness once and for all, having already had quite an eventful time since arriving back in their own time as it was.

The plan was simple enough, at least in theory. They would use the rift to rejoin their own timeline, at the only location available to them, Marvin's workshop. Gambling on the fact that Forrester would have insisted the generators remained constantly operational until his return, in case of emergencies. Because they had the timephone with them, Forrester would be unable to use it to anchor the far end of the wormhole to their present day.

Frank had needed all his powers of concentration, somewhat anathema to a man so adept at ignoring all but the most immediate of his surroundings, to grasp even Hannah's simplified explanation of this part of the plan. But she thought it was important he understood they were returning to the same hostile situation they had left and Forrester would have more than likely stationed men to guard the workshop.

At this, Frank brightened considerably, knowing his area of expertise when he heard it and assuring Hannah he was "fully capable of making snap operational decisions and performing tactical risk assessments in the field", a phrase he recited with the faraway look of a man clawing something back from the furthest reaches of memory.

Hannah realised, with a pang of grief and a stronger flare of anger, that it was one of the things Bronk had jokingly taught the henchman-turned-security consultant, and Frank had clearly taken it to heart. It just made her more determined that they make it through this alive if only to give some meaning to the death of the strange little man who was largely responsible for her still being alive and whom she missed terribly, much to her own surprise.

And surprise had certainly been on their side when they materialized on the makeshift landing platform in Marvin's workshop.

The two guards had obviously become complacent after waiting for so long without any clear orders or leadership and were sitting together playing cards at a steel-topped laboratory table adrift with empty beer cans, overflowing ashtrays and scattered pizza boxes when Hannah, then Frank, snap, crackled and popped into existence right in front of their eyes.

One of the advantages of Frank's previously explored ability, to not think about even the most appalling things, was that he seemed all but immune to the disorienting effects of temporal distortion. This meant that as soon as he appeared behind Hannah, who was on all fours, groaning and trying her best not to think of jellied eels, Frank was ready for action and launched himself at the unsuspecting guards before they had time to react.

Frank took out the man nearest to him as he reached the table, simply by bringing Marvin's stout wooden box down on the startled guard's head. He fell face down in a half-eaten pizza while his partner was scrabbling for his gun amongst the detritus on the table. A foolish waste of valuable seconds, which could have been far more sensibly spent putting as much distance between himself and Furious Frank as possible.

The guard was desperately trying to push his chair back from the table and stand up, Hannah remembered with an involuntary shudder, when the rear chair legs had come up against the edge of an uneven floorboard and he had started to topple over backwards.

Frank charged at the heavy steel table and shoved it into the already unstable man, knocking him flat on his back, then lifting the table and overturning it, the leading edge slamming down onto the trapped man's throat.

It wasn't strictly Frank's fault that the table was heavier than it looked, he just didn't know his own strength sometimes. But that didn't make Hannah feel any better, as the image once more flashed across her memory; the guard's head, eyes wide open in a comical expression of shock, rolling to a stop in front of her, sliced neatly off by Frank's improvised guillotine. Hannah shook herself, forcing her mind back to the present.

They had disabled the generator nearly two hours ago, and Frank had taken a large spanner to some of the more fragile and intricate-looking components. The resulting destruction was enough to keep even Marvin Calderwood himself busy for several days. Now it was just a matter of location, timing and hoping Marvin would stick to the plan.

Frank had searched the pockets of the two deceased goons and found a set of keys to the car parked outside, so they were able to hit the road soon after, but not before Frank rigged some sort of improvised self-destruct device.

As the Mercedes 4×4 drove away from the building, an explosion shook the car on its suspension and Hannah turned to see flames and thick, black smoke belching from the windows of Marvin's workshop. She looked over at Frank, whose face was set in a careful poker face. "Gas leak, you think, Frank?"

"Gotta be, yeah, lucky we got out really. Just goes to show, you never can tell…"

Five minutes later they passed a sign for Bristol: 90 miles.

Hannah checked the contents of the wooden box at her feet for the umpteenth time, making sure the little red light on the charger cable plugged into the dashboard still glowed steadily. She wouldn't be able to live with herself if she failed to save the world from a ruinous, global financial dictatorship because of a flat battery on her phone.

Marvin was dozing in his chair, his pepperpot revolver on the desk in front of him, some three and a half hours after Hannah and Frank had vanished into the shimmering silver portal when he was jarred awake by the sound of violent hammering on the door to the street.

"Come on Calderwood, you can't protect that Meredith bitch forever!" More hammering. "I'm going to get in there sooner or later, you treacherous old bastard. And when I do, I'm going to gut you like a fish!"

The voice had a mad, manic tone to it, one that Marvin had only heard a few times in all his dealings with the despicable Paul Forrester and he knew it only meant one thing, Forrester was just about ready to go over the edge.

Marvin Calderwood looked at his watch, picked up the revolver and trained it on the door at the top of the basement steps, sighting down the stubby barrel to see he had a clear shot from his desk, just in case. Then he sat back and tried to ignore the increasingly obscene threats being screamed through the door.

"I think we'll let you stew another half an hour yet, Mr. Forrester, sir." Marvin grinned, with no humour whatsoever. "Then you can come in and I'll do exactly what you want, I give you my word on it."

32
The Noose Tightens

If If Hannah was nervous or having second thoughts, Frank couldn't see any sign of it, as he watched her lean against the front of the car, smoking a cigarette and gazing at the spectacular view as the sun set behind the hills on the other side of the Avon gorge.

They had been parked in a layby on the outskirts of Bristol for nearly an hour and she'd barely said a word since leaving Marvin's workshop that afternoon. Something of a record for Hannah, who was usually far too chatty for Frank's social skills to cope with and anyway, their conversations almost always ended up with Hannah taking the piss and Frank sulking, so he had been enjoying the break.

But now he was, if not exactly worried - worrying was another thing Frank's highly specialised psyche had long ago de-prioritised as being a waste of its limited resources - then at least he was aware of the need to keep an eye on her. She was a woman, of course, thought Frank, you never knew what women were going to do next. Well, he certainly didn't, and that was what currently mattered to Frank, because it was her plan but he was the one who had to carry it out and that made him... concerned.

In a professional capacity, you understand.

He would have liked to have been consulted, obviously. He was the Head of Security in this outfit, after all, but the look in her eye when she told him what was going to happen, well, it didn't seem a good time to question her reasoning, that was all. It's not like he had a better plan, so Frank let it be. He just hoped Bronk's death hadn't pushed her over the edge, suicide missions were not what Frank had signed up for.

Marvin checked the readout on the power gauge of the main generator and seemed satisfied with what he saw. He muttered something to himself and scribbled a note on the scrap of paper he was holding, adding to a list of figures that would have been meaningless to anyone else, without knowing Marvin's unique form of personal shorthand. He then returned to the control console and consulted his scrawled calculations as he carefully readjusted the settings, grimacing as Forrester made a renewed assault on the basement door, for all the good it would do him.

Before he'd left, Frank had fashioned a device which he had referred to as a "raid lock", a metal rod attached to the door and jammed into a hole chiselled into the stone floor, making it impossible for anyone to get in without some serious mechanical assistance.

"You think you can stay in there forever, Calderwood?" shouted Forrester through the stout timbers of the door, "If I have to spend the rest of my life in this primitive shithole, then so be it, but I will kill you if I do, you can depend on that."

Marvin looked at his watch and realised he couldn't put it off any longer, it was time to initiate the final stage of Hannah's plan. Or the final part he would play in it, at least, and he was determined not to let her down.

He checked the settings on the console once more and slowly powered down the generator, watching the silvery portal, like a magical mirror suspended in the air, fizzle out at the end of the lab before turning off the arc lights which surrounded the space where it hung.

Marvin looked around one final time, making sure he hadn't forgotten anything, then he crossed the basement, stood for a moment to see if his heart was going to slow its galloping beat, decided that it probably wasn't and began climbing the steps to the door.

Hannah got back in the car and looked at Frank. "All clear on what we're doing, Frank?"

No shake in her voice, no break in eye contact, he thought, that's good.

"Marvin should be letting Forrester in about now, so it won't be long before this will all be over."

He nodded and gave a noncommittal shrug. "One way or another, yeah, fings are gonna end badly for someone."

"That's what I'm going to miss about you, Frank, your endless supply of optimism and positivity." She grinned and a spark of the Hannah that Frank had come to sort-of-admire shone in her eyes for a second, reassuring him somewhat as to her mental state. "But don't you concern yourself with anything, I'm sure everything is going to go according to plan. We've gotten this far, haven't we?"

"I'll give you that." Frank replied grudgingly.

"Me 'n' Toby, we reckoned you'd be a quick lunchtime job before we snuck off for a couple of cheeky pints on the way home." He rubbed his injured arm absently. "And look how that fucking turned out, Toby's a stiff and I've turned into Doctor bleedin' Who."

Frank shook his head sadly. "It wasn't like this back in the old days, we didn't 'ave no time travelling master criminals back then, it was just yer normal breaking kneecaps, offing the competition, you know, general muscle and doorman type stuff..?"

"I'm not sure that I do, Frank," favouring him with one of her best sardonic expressions, which was encouraging in itself, "but I'll accept your professional analysis on the relative merits of your past employment and I can only apologise that your current arrangement isn't entirely to your liking." She smiled sweetly at him and patted his arm. "Please feel free to register your feedback with HR at your exit interview."

"Ha fucking ha," going for grumpy but unable to suppress a crooked grin, "I'll be wanting a sodding bonus, I'll tell you that for fuck all."

"Your severance package will be suitably generous, I'll be sure to see to it. Now, it's time we got going, you know what to do." She climbed out of the car and reached down to pick up the wooden box, the hastily scratched word Stuff just visible on the side and paused, her hand on the door. "Oh, and Frank," he looked over at her as he started the engine, "good luck."

Then she closed the door, tucked the box under her arm and began to jog up the road in the slowly gathering shadows of dusk, out onto the historic span of the Clifton suspension bridge, for her final showdown with Paul Forrester.

Marvin took a deep breath and banged on the door with his fist, "Can you hear me, Forrester?"

The sneer in Forrester's voice was clear, even through the door. "I'm here, did you think I'd gone away? What do you want?"

"If I let you in, what guarantee do I have that you won't just kill me?" Marvin's hand rested on Frank's DIY barricade device. "I want your assurance that neither I, nor my family, are to be harmed or harassed in any way from now on. If you give me your word on that, I will open the door."

"I have no interest in you or your miserable family anymore, Calderwood," said Forrester with irritation, "just get me back where I came from and you'll never see me again."

Marvin was careful to stay silent for a moment before answering, to let Forrester know he was considering his offer. "Alright Forrester, stand away from the door." As an afterthought, he added, "I should warn you that I am armed and I shall not hesitate to shoot if you attempt any treachery."

"Haha, you're perfectly safe, Marvin," laughed Forrester, "I'm only interested in that bitch, Meredith, I won't try any heroics, don't worry."

Marvin pulled on the iron bar as Frank had shown him and, sure enough, the brace easily slid free, allowing him to open the door.

Forrester stood a few feet from the open door, his arms held away from his body in a non-threatening posture, an innocent expression on his face and waited for Marvin to invite him inside.

Marvin came out and moved round behind him, gingerly patting his sides in an ineffectual search for weapons, then prodded him towards the doorway with the barrel of his revolver.

They went down the steps into the laboratory and Forrester stopped after a few steps and rounded on Marvin angrily. "What is this, where's the portal?" he gestured round the dimly lit basement, "If you think you can double cross me, old man…"

"Calm down, Forrester," said Marvin, in a patient tone, "I had to power down the generator after Miss Meredith returned to her own time, to prevent the feedback coil transponder from overheating." Marvin was rather pleased with himself at this piece of improvised techno-babble, especially since Forrester seemed to accept it as an explanation and watched silently as Marvin went through the start up procedure on the generators.

"Where did you send them?" he asked, after Marvin finally looked up from the controls and nodded.

"The only place I could send them," said Marvin, perfectly truthfully, "to my workshop where, I sincerely hope, you left my machines running, when you left to come here."

"I did," replied Forrester with a grin that Marvin didn't like one bit, "and the whole place was heavily guarded by some of my best men, so I'm guessing that she is already dead or, if they know what's good for them, they've saved her for me to…play with, before I kill her."

Marvin looked at him with unveiled disgust but didn't respond, he just pointed to the end of the room and threw a switch to turn on the arc lamps. "Go and stand over there, but don't go past the marker," he pointed to a rough line painted on the wall and smiled pleasantly, "if you know what's good for you."

Forrester watched as Marvin turned the power dial on the console and was aware that the hairs on the back of his neck were standing up and he could suddenly smell ozone.

The next thing he knew, the rift blinked open in front of him and the same crackling, hissing noise he remembered from the woods filled the room.

"Well, Marvin," he said raising a hand in the old scientist's direction, "it's been a pleasure doing business with you. But now, I fear I must bid you adieu." Then Paul Forrester spread his arms and walked into the shimmering, swirling portal for the last time and vanished.

33
Endgame

Hannah paused for a moment and shifted the wooden box into a more comfortable position under her arm. She looked through the iron framework of the bridge, down into the shadowy depths of the Avon Gorge, then up at the inscription on the support tower which loomed over her in the quickly fading light; "SUSPENSA VIX VIA FIT". Hannah frowned as she trawled her memory for half-forgotten schoolgirl Latin and decided it was something like "The road becomes barely suspended".

"Sounds like the bloody wormhole," she said to herself, "A - B in the blink of an eye, with nothing to support you but a tunnel of light."

She passed under the giant stone arch and headed out onto the "barely suspended" road, seeing the cliffs fall away steeply beneath her, the densely wooded sides plunging 250 feet to the river below and the wind becoming stronger, the closer she got to the centre of the gorge.

Cars were passing her with less regularity, now that the rush hour traffic had dwindled to a few late office workers and long distance commuters on the last leg of their journey home. Not that she was worried about being seen, dark shadows cast by a three quarter moon, now brightly visible in the eastern sky ahead and to her left, combined with her dark clothes, meant that she was all but invisible if she kept close to the iron latticework that made up the sides of the bridge.

Hannah glanced at her watch, realised she had less than five minutes until the deadline they had agreed with

Marvin and quickened her pace. After a minute or so she looked back the way she had come, then turned and looked ahead of her and estimated she was roughly halfway across, above the deepest part of the gorge. When she was sure there were no other pedestrians around, Hannah knelt and placed the box on the pavement, opened the lid and took out the wired together phones, which she immediately switched on. She waited for a few seconds until the reception indicator on her mobile phone showed there was a strong signal, then reached in and removed the rest of the box's contents and closed the lid.

Aided by shafts of moonlight filtering through the crisscross metalwork of the bridge, Hannah consulted a rumpled scrap of paper she had taken from the pocket of her jeans and carefully used the dial on the timephone to enter the coordinates, written by Marvin in his unnecessarily flowery, old fashioned cursive handwriting.

She checked the connecting cable and settings twice, just to be sure, glanced once more in each direction then, taking a deep breath, Hannah punched the "connect" button.

Frank had driven over the bridge, passing Hannah before she even reached the support tower and watched her figure being swallowed by the darkness in his rearview mirror, then found a place where he could turn the Mercedes around and wait. He had offered to drop her off halfway across, but she said the walk would help calm her nerves and that had been that.

Now Frank climbed out of the car and began walking back towards the middle of the bridge from the opposite end, keeping to the shadows like Hannah and occasionally glancing over his shoulder to make sure he was alone. When he was almost at the mid-point of the bridge, the rising wind whipping at his clothes, Frank raised the night vision goggles he had taken from Forrester's man in the woods and trained them on the pavement ahead of him.

Sure enough, Hannah's ghostly green image swam into focus and he watched as she made some adjustments to Marvin's weird contraption before sitting down with her back against Brunel's intricate ironwork and lighting one of those stinking cheroots she was so fond of, the tip glowing fiercely through the enhanced binoculars as she waited.

Frank crouched down and waited with her. "Not long now, you bastard," he growled, "and then you're gonna get what's fucking coming to you."

As soon as Marvin saw the indicator light flicker into life on the console, he knew Hannah had managed to activate the chronophonic device successfully, meaning that the rift would have a stable anchor point in the future and Forrester would arrive as expected. He just hoped she remembered to adjust the settings, otherwise, the plan might all be for nothing.

The moment Forrester vanished through the shimmering silver portal, Marvin checked the generators were all running smoothly and reset the dials on the console to match those he had given Hannah before she left. Then he began shifting the scattered workbenches, chairs and odd pieces of scientific equipment in the laboratory so they were against the walls, leaving a clear path from the circle of arc lamps where the rift opened, all the way down the length of the basement to the stone wall at the far end.

For Paul Forrester's part, his second journey through the rift was considerably more comfortable than his first without a brain-dead thug trying to rip his head off this time. So he had little reason to doubt Marvin's word when he had promised Forrester would be returning to the safety of the foolish old man's workshop and was therefore unprepared for what he found as his journey abruptly ended.

The first indication that all was not as it should be was the fact that it was dark, there was a strong wind blowing and there was a very definite feeling of... nothing, immediately to his left.

The second indication was the sound of that bloody Meredith woman's voice, startling him as she spoke from just behind him.

"Oh, you made it, good. I'm so glad you could join us."

Paul Forrester stood very still and waited with interest to see what would happen next.

Hannah stubbed out her cheroot and stood up. She peered down the bridge in each direction, her gaze lingering slightly longer to the east as if she could sense Frank's presence in the darkness, watching over her, waiting for his big moment.

"Right, this is it then," said Hannah Meredith in a decisive voice, to the world in general, "time to stop all this bloody lunacy and get my life back."

Bending down, she picked up the wooden box with the connected phones on top of it, reached above her head and placed it onto the sturdy iron balustrade beside her, then, with a final anxious glance into the dark, Hannah clambered up onto the narrow iron parapet just in time.

The familiar, tinny smell of ozone filled the air and, where there had been nothing only a split second before, the silver disc of the rift was suddenly just there, without going through all the complicated business of actually materialising in front of her eyes or anything as clichéd as that, one instant it wasn't there, the next, there it was.

She was surprised at first because Forrester emerged through the other side of the disc, the one that faced away from her and she didn't see him for a second. Then the shining portal winked out of existence in the same disconcerting way it had appeared and Hannah found herself two steps behind her nemesis, just one ill-advised sidestep from the edge of the abyss.

"Oh, you made it, good. I'm so glad you could join us."

There was no response from Forrester, he just stood there, but Hannah could tell he was tensed, alert to any threat.

"I expect you thought you'd end up in Marvin's nice cozy workshop, didn't you, Paul?" she asked. "Sorry, your goons suffered a nasty case of Frank. One of them really lost his head over the whole thing, I'm afraid. But that's ok, no hard feelings, eh?"

She waited, still nothing. "Why don't you turn round, Mr. Forrester," Hannah didn't like looking at the back of his head, she couldn't tell what he was thinking, "I believe I have something you want."

Forrester gave no sign that he'd even heard her speak, let alone that he would do as she asked, so, keeping her eyes locked on his back, Hannah bent forward, as if reaching for the box that lay on the parapet between them.

It was the only chance Forrester needed. He spun round to face Hannah, at the same time lunging for the tangled mass of wires and electronic devices on top of the box.

He felt his fingers close on the body of Marvin's incredible invention and snatched it away from Hannah who, apparently shocked by his lightning reactions, was only now reaching for the empty wooden box, as Forrester smiled in triumph, took a step back from her and looked down at his prize. "What the..?"

Forrester's head snapped up, in time to see Hannah lift the timephone from the open box, smile the least amusing smile he'd ever seen and press a small red button. Unable to help himself, he looked down at the what he held in his hands, finally recognising it for what it was; a cheap disposable phone, a collection of random components, hurriedly assembled and connected to each other in a useless tangle of wires.

"Not what you were expecting?" Hannah's voice was now totally devoid of emotion, a monotone. "Sorry, I must have got some of Bronk's junk mixed up in the box. You remember Bronk? He died because of you, you pig."

She held up the timephone. "He kept this away from you though, didn't he, you megalomaniac bastard? Well, now it's time for you to pay the price for your greed." Hannah suddenly held the phones out over the side of the bridge and dangled them by the connecting cable, "I tell you what, why don't you come and get them?"

When the phone rang.

Forrester didn't wait to see what would happen next, he used the moment of surprise and rushed forward in a last attempt to grab Hannah and regain control of the situation. But she didn't react the way he expected, in fact, she didn't react at all. Instead of trying to back away or escape, she just stood and watched him come at her and Forrester didn't notice anything wrong until it was too late.

Frank, who had crept silently along the path until he was directly below them, rose up from the side of the bridge like a vengeful golem with anger issues and slammed into Forrester, knocking him down and sending him sprawling towards the edge.

"Now!" Frank bellowed to Hannah, as Forrester scrabbled for grip on the slippery iron and slid closer to the edge.

Hannah saw Forrester go down and heard Frank yell at the same time. She didn't hesitate, she dropped the phones back into the box with the word Stuff faintly scratched on the side, then simply threw the whole lot over the side.

Frank looked down into Forrester's eyes, as he hung by his fingers from a jagged metal bracket on the safety rail, then looked past him, down into the gorge and saw the bloom of light he'd been expecting.

"This is for Mr. Bronk."

Frank stamped down hard, once, on the blood-slippery hand and coldly watched Paul Forrester fall into the abyss.

Forrester felt a searing pain in his hand and let go.

He fell, in darkness, weightless.

He heard the wind roaring past and tried to scream, but the volume of air being forced into his lungs made it impossible.

Then he saw the gleaming circle of light speeding toward him and in that split second he realised what was going to happen, he was going straight through the portal. Hannah had caused the rift to open in midair and he was falling into it at something approaching a hundred miles an hour.

Marvin heard the telltale crackling fizz of the portal opening and looked up from his desk.

Less than five seconds later, the gently rippling, mirrored surface exploded violently outwards and a large object exited the rift with incredible force, flew down the length of the basement and slammed into the wall with a grisly crunching noise and an extraordinary amount of blood.

Marvin waited until he was sure nothing else was coming through and then, with shaking hands, he turned off the power to the generators, picked up the mop and bucket he had ready and set to work clearing up the mess.

34
Epilogue

"Paula, could you come in here, please." DCI Philip Ryland released the intercom button, then, as an afterthought, he punched it again. "Oh, and Paula, bring my diary in with you, please."

It was only Tuesday and he felt worn out. "You're getting old, Phil," he muttered to himself, "forgetting stuff is just par for the course from now on."

Ryland shook his head and looked up from the headline that blared from the tabloid on his desk; "**DID ALIENS VISIT BRISTOL? STRANGE LIGHTS SPOTTED IN AVON GORGE**" as Paula, his secretary came into the office.

"Ah, Paula," he said, frowning uncertainty, "stupid question, but wasn't I working on a case...?" He tailed off, frustration darkening his already weary expression as she looked at him with curiosity

"I know, I know," Ryland said, irritably, "that's not a lot to go on... It's just..." He rubbed his forehead, then leaned forward with his eyes screwed tightly shut, sitting like that for long enough that Paula started to think he'd had some sort of fit. "I have a nagging feeling we were getting close to someone, some villain called... Frost..? No, no that's not right..." He opened his eyes and looked up, to see if any of this had jogged her memory. "...Foster..? Forster..?"

Ryland gave Paula a helpless look, "None of this means anything to you, does it?"

"Not really, sir," she replied, looking at her boss with a mixture of amusement and mild, professional concern.

"Maybe if you could give me a little more to go on?" She nevertheless flicked through the last week or so of his appointments and case log, but found nothing and shook her head at him. "No reference to anyone with a name even close to that in your diary, it's been a pretty quiet week, I'd have thought you'd be glad of the rest."

"That's just it," Ryland said with a sigh, "I just thought..." Again he failed to articulate the feeling of a memory, tantalizingly out of reach and fading fast. "It seemed really important earlier and I almost remembered what it was about, but it could just be my mind playing tricks on me, maybe I got it mixed up with another case. I have been overdoing it a bit recently, I should probably take some time off."

"That's probably it, yes," Paula agreed, glad the strange expression was clearing from DCI Ryland's face, "book a week off and potter around the garden, it'll do you the world of good."

She was right, he thought, that sounded like a very tempting idea. "You know what, I think I might do just that." he smiled, feeling better already, "Thanks Paula, I don't know what I'd do without you."

Marvin Calderwood watched through the small glass panel in the door, until the tightly wrapped canvas bundle had been utterly consumed by the roaring flames.

He turned to George, an old friend who worked as a caretaker at the university and didn't ask too many questions when Marvin needed to "borrow" a piece of scientific equipment for the weekend or, in this case, "dispose of the result of a failed experiment" in the furnace.

"Thank you, George," he said, pressing some cash into the old man's hand, "you've saved me a great deal of embarrassment, trying to explain my failure to such an important client."

Whether George saw through the lie or not, Marvin couldn't say, but he knew they had an understanding and his friend had a conveniently unreliable memory when it came to such things, so he was confident he had heard the last of the abominable Paul Forrester and all those associated with him.

Driving his carriage home, Marvin couldn't help wondering if Hannah had been able to extricate herself from Forrester's despicable organisation quite so easily. He hoped so because he thought it extremely unlikely that he would ever find out for sure.

Hannah sat in the passenger seat of the Mercedes, the car Frank had taken as one of the "spoils of war", as he'd so eloquently put it, looking out of the window at the countryside speeding past and considered what she'd been through in the last few days.

She was lucky to be alive, she was certain of that, but there weren't too many other things she could say with the same certainty. She didn't see how Forrester could have survived, as long as everything had worked the way she planned it with Marvin. Even Frank, who she sat down with last night and explained, as best she could, the need for it to have been done the way it was, had finally accepted that the extra risk made sense, once he was in full possession of the facts. Or at least as many facts as Frank could successfully retain at any given moment.

The reason, she explained in the simplest way possible, that they couldn't have just "chucked the fucker off the bridge and be done with it", as Frank had advised, or just have Forrester materialize out of the rift over thin air and watch him plummet to the bottom of the gorge, was because it was essential that Forrester died in the past.

As Hannah understood the theory of it - hurriedly

explained by Marvin following Bronk's death, after he saw the dead look in her eyes - as soon as Forrester died, back in Victorian London, he would have ceased to exist as part of her past as she perceived it, back here in the present day.

This meant as he was erased from history, along with the patent applications Marvin had burned with his mangled remains, all he had done to affect the passage of time during his life would also immediately vanish, leaving no trace of the man who set the events in motion. He would likewise disappear from people's memories, even those who had been directly involved with him.

Hannah had been fully prepared for her memory of the whole insane affair to vanish, along with those of everyone else, but Marvin assured her the trips she had made through the rift would somehow insulate her from this amnesiac side effect and it appeared that, so far at least, he was right.

The one thing, or rather the one person Hannah wished she could forget was, strangely, not the man who had devoted so much time and energy to completely and utterly destroying her, but the one who had saved her life more times than she could count, ultimately at the cost of his own.

Whenever she thought about Bronk, she felt a loss she found hard to reconcile with a man she had known for so short a time and who had helped her without any thought for his own safety, so she pushed these feelings aside until she could explore them more thoroughly.

Frank was just, well, Frank.

None of what had gone on at the bridge had phased him in the slightest and he was now his normal, slablike and sardonic self, driving with an economical but aggressive style, which seemed to signal subliminally to other road users that they should get out of his way or face the consequences.

They were heading back to Hannah's place, with a half concocted, half true story about her miraculous escape from murderous burglars and her rescue by good Samaritan, Frank, who had picked her up at the side of the road as she fled from her attackers and kept her out of harm's way until she judged it safe to return.

With any luck, all the evidence that tied her to events surrounding Forrester and his band of merry mercenaries would have vanished, along with all links to Hannah and any... questionable activities on her part.

She had agreed to keep Frank around at the farmhouse, just for a while anyway, until she was sure any threat from Forrester's little cabal had passed, on a salary that was still to be negotiated.

And that appeared to be that; even though nothing could have prepared her for such an incredible adventure, she had beaten the odds and survived. She didn't plan on getting involved in anything even remotely similar, ever again, all Hannah wanted was to return to her quiet and boring life in the country.

Happy to have made this momentous decision, she had just decided she might try and sleep the rest of the way home, when they passed a sign which read:

**ESTATE SALE: TODAY AT THE ROYAL OAK INN, ANDOVER.
BY PUBLIC AUCTION.
EVERYTHING MUST GO!**

Hannah Meredith looked at her watch, realised she hadn't eaten anything since sometime back in the nineteenth century and turned to her chauffeur.

"Frank, do you fancy a drink?"

About the Author

Guy Thair is older than you think and lives in the beautiful North Devon countryside with his wife and daughter.

He began writing fiction on his blog in 2015, using weekly prompts from other bloggers to inspire short stories. This unconventional approach to writing suited him so well he accidentlly wrote a whole novel the same way.

Oh, and he doesn't own a computer, so he does all of his writing from his phone.

If you enjoyed this story, please consider taking a few moments to write a review on GoodReads.

You can use the QR Code below to take you directly there.

17655324R00117

Printed in Great Britain
by Amazon